THE MEME PLAGUE

MEMENTO NORA

THE MEME PLAGUE

BY ANGIE SMIBERT

SKYSCAPE

SKYSCAPE

Text copyright © 2013 by Angela Smibert

Library of Congress Cataloging-in-Publication Data is available upon request.
ISBN-13: 9781477816608 (hardcover)
ISBN-10: 1477816607 (hardcover)
ISBN-13: 9781477866603 (eBook)
ISBN-10: 1477866604 (eBook)

Book design by Alex Ferrari
Editor: Marilyn Brigham

Printed in the United States of America (R)
First edition
10 9 8 7 6 5 4 3 2 1

To everyone who believed: my friends, family, fans, critique partners, agent, and especially my editor, Marilyn, who believed enough to take a chance on Nora in the first place.

MemeCast 2.0—

WHAT YOU DID ON YOUR SUMMER VACATION

Okay, citizens. This is obviously not Meme Girl. Call me Meme, uh, Boy for now. Summer's over. School starts tomorrow. And you have forgotten more than you know.

Yeah, we all forget stuff over the summer: the names of Henry VIII's wives, how to solve a quadratic equation, what makes the noble gases so darn noble.

But you've forgotten much more than how to solve for X or that krypton is a real element. And you can't blame the old forgetting curve. (Who studies over the summer anyway?)

Nope. You, my friend, have been hacked.

Someone made you forget. More than just your cares. Yes, TFC—and our fine mayor and his Patriot Party cronies—have strategically wiped certain events from your wetware. Maybe you were a victim of an old-fashioned, brute force hack. TFC's security—Soft Target, or Green Zone, or General Zod, or whatever lamesauce name they're calling themselves now—picked you up in a black van or even a police car. They took you to Detention. AKA, the Big D. There you spilled your guts about whatever, swallowed the Big Pill, and went on your merry way. Minus a few key memories. Maybe they gaslighted you into thinking you were in the hospital or juvenile hall.

Or maybe you succumbed to TFC's newer, stealthier hack. A Trojan horse. Remember those ID chips Mayor Mignon required us to get this summer? He said they'd keep us safe. Well, TFC slipped a little something else into that chip.

It could all be part of a power play to rig the vote for this fall's election or something even more dastardly. Who really knows?

Okay, back to the hackage. What data did you lose?

If I told you everything, it might fill a couple of books. But here are the CliffsNotes:

At the end of the school year, three Hamilton kids discovered that TFC was behind some of the car bombings in our fair city, and they put it all in a series of underground comics.

They got caught and were sent—along with some family and friends—to Detention where they had their brains bleached the old-fashioned way.

But not everyone got caught. Meme Girl, a reporter who'd covered the story, started this underground radio show, the MemeCast, to keep us informed about what was really going on.

During the summer, the mayor announced that everyone had to have these new implanted ID chips. And many other cities decided to do the same thing. (You know this part.)

Turns out the chips could be used to implant memories, not just erase them.

But my friends and I figured out a way to clean the malware off your chip—at least temporarily. Our plan involved broadcasting a certain concert over the Meme-Cast. Embedded in that 'cast was a program that erased the implanted memories on the ID chips.

It worked, but not without causalities of the memory variety. Meme Girl and many others at the rave got picked up, including someone I'd come to like very much.

That was July.

It's now September, and we've got a lot to do before Election Day.

Fight the hack, citizens. Take a tip from a friend of mine: Remind yourself what you know to be true. I'll try to help with that.

Next up: Agent Smith's cover of a not-so-moldy oldie, "Everybody Wants to Rule the World."

1.0

FUNERAL FOR THE PAST

MICAH WALLENBERG

Ah, Labor Day—and the end of mine. Labors, that is. I'd just lugged my last box of canned corn and ravioli for the summer. My community service sentence for something I didn't remember doing.

And it didn't matter that what "they" told me I did and what I really did were not the same thing. Those few weeks in May (and some in June) were still a blank.

But I trusted my friends more than the Therapeutic Forgetting Clinic Corporation—and this chip in my head.

On my way, I texted Nora. I took a good whiff of my pits and added, *after I shower*. Then I crammed a cherry Pop-Tart in my mouth, dropped my board to the sidewalk, and kicked off toward home—our new one. Black Dog Village was dust, but we had a shiny new apartment, courtesy of "them." AKA, TFC. I had zero say in the matter. Mom signed us up for their Rehousing Program when I was in "juvie." That was what "they" called it. I knew now that I'd never been in juvie. I was in Detention. The Big D variety.

Shifting the weight of my backpack as I leaned into the turn, I banked around the corner of Market and First Streets. Mr. Jeffries had loaded me up before I left the food bank. He knew our situation.

TFC cares about the concerns of our less fortunate citizens, a little voice whispered in the depths of my brain.

I kicked off hard, trying to clear my head as I glided through the familiar streets of downtown. As I passed boarded-up shop after shop, I repeated to myself what I *knew* to be true. It was my own personal Therapeutic Forgetting Clinic experience—in reverse. Repetition made the last three months seem more real in my head.

One. Me, Winter, and a girl named Nora (whom I've crushed on all year from afar) got busted for distributing an underground comic about TFC and its less than savory practices—like blowing up cars and who knows what other shit.

Two.

My front wheels caught a chunk of concrete, and I nearly face-planted onto the sidewalk and into a pile of rubble. A wave of déjà vu washed over me as I lay there for a second. I'd taken my fair share of hits on a board. In fact, I'd just gotten a cast off my arm a few months before. I pushed myself up to my knees and took stock. Nothing broken, though my elbows looked like hamburger. Then I noticed where I was.

In front of Fahrenheit Books—or what was left of it.

Someone had spray-painted "Memento" in red across the big FOR SALE sign. This is where it all started. According to Nora's mom. This was where Nora saw the body. If she hadn't been here when the store blew up, she and I might never have met in TFC number 23. Or so we've been told.

Something dripped down my back, and it smelled like pickles.

Sure enough, the jar of dill slices had cracked, and the juice was all over the place. *I don't even like pickles.* I pulled out the cans of tuna, chili, and creamed corn and then dumped the pickles and broken glass out into the gutter. The rest of the Pop-Tarts smelled like pickles, too. Crap.

As I was sitting on my can stuffing the groceries back into my pack, somebody walked by. I jumped to my feet, grabbing both my pack and board, just in case it was a cop. My homeless habits die hard.

It wasn't a cop. It was a guy dressed in a black suit— with a top hat—carrying a long box. Written on the side of the gray box, which I swear was in the shape of a casket, was the word HISTORY in bright red.

Behind this guy was a fairly long procession of other people in black all carrying their own mini-caskets. And they were all as silent as—well, a funeral. Most folks weren't decked out like the first guy. A girl in a black hoodie carried a box that said MEMORY. An older guy in a black T-shirt carried one that said PRIVACY. Next was FREE SPEECH. LIBERTY. There were even ones for MEMECAST and MEMENTO. Then came people's names: FRANK B., CECILIA H., JOSE R., SARAH J.

I didn't get it. *Are these people dead? Are these ideas dead?* MemeCast hadn't exactly flat-lined, but I hadn't drawn a frame of *Memento* since I literally couldn't remember when.

The name on the last casket was JONAS W.

My pack slipped from my fingers, and I stared after the procession as it disappeared around the next corner.

It couldn't be. There have to be zillions of Jonas W's in the world, right? They can't be talking about Jonas Wallenberg. My dad.

I dropped my skateboard to the sidewalk and caught up to the mock funeral on the next block. The people were headed toward TFC No. 23.

Now it made a little more sense. TFC erased memories. Each person inside TFC No. 23 was popping a little white pill to forget a memory that was haunting them. They might have seen a Coalition bombing, gotten beaten by their husband, or been hit by a car. Forgetting wasn't necessarily a bad thing, Mom always said.

Would she still think that if *she'd* been to the Big D?

The thought struck me. *My dad could be in Detention.*

Not that I hadn't considered the possibility before. It sucks that I couldn't remember what happened to him. All I had of him was this recurring nightmare of losing him in a crowd.

The lead funeral guy laid his casket in front of the clinic's glossy glass door. The other mourners did the same. The people inside the TFC pressed their faces up against the glass to watch the show.

I hung back across the street.

The guy in the top hat pulled out a piece of paper and started to read, "Dearly beloved, we are gathered here today to mourn the loss of . . ."

He was quickly drowned out by the wail of sirens approaching. The city cops blocked off the streets but stayed in their cars, lights flashing. Then a black van roared in, and goons in Green Zone uniforms poured out. They were TFC's own private army of cops.

I melted into the shadows of a doorway. Most people on the street ducked into other buildings or hustled off down alleys. *I really should do that, too,* I thought, but I was glued to the spot, unable not to watch.

A city police car rolled slowly past me. One window slid down, and the cop yelled at me, "Run, kid!" She quickly closed the window—and pulled on a gas mask.

Without a word, the Green Zone cops let loose a barrage of some kind of canisters—right at the mourners. Point blank. The people in black—men, women, and kids my age—crumpled to their knees in a cloud of gas.

The real cops didn't even get out of their cars.

I ran like hell, my eyes and throat burning all the way home.

No amount of hot water can wash away today, I told myself as I tore off my clothes and practically dived into the shower.

Forget your cares at TFC, a little voice whispered in my head.

Hot water pounded my face as I recited what I knew to be true.

One.

2.0

THE MISUNDER-ESTIMATION OF VELVET KOWALCYK

VELVET KOWALCYK

I rapped on 4D, hoping for another no answer.

We were knocking on our last doors before the big rally on the first day of school. Most of the summer we'd hit up the large compounds: Los Palamos, Tamarind Bay, Hunting Hills, and Laguna Woods. Today we were in the "TFC projects," as my minder liked to call them.

This was my community service for the rave. I'd been charged with breaking curfew and trespassing. The judge evidently had a sense of humor, making me "volunteer" for Mayor Mignon's congressional campaign. The rave had definitely been *anti*-Mignon in flavor.

Just as we were ready to move on, Micah answered the door. In a towel. Trying to keep a straight face, I gave my spiel and pressed a flyer into his free hand. He stood there gawking at me like I'd undergone some complete personality transformation just because I wasn't dressed in my usual vintage-punk splendor.

Clothes don't define me. *Book of Velvet*. Verse 1, Chapter 1.

Admittedly, this ensemble was lame. I had on a yellow (yuck) Albert Mignon T-shirt, jeans, and sneakers. My plain brown hair was pulled back into a stubby ponytail. *I* wouldn't have recognized me, but, hey, I was just doing my time. And the Mignon folks weren't too thrilled when I rocked up the first day in my ratty Anthrax tee, mini-skirt, striped leggings, combat boots, and blue hair. In fact, I got an extra day added onto my sentence for it.

My "big sister," Buffy McCheerleader (not her real name), rolled her eyes at Micah clutching his towel, which barely covered his skinny white butt. Poor guy looked like he'd had a rough day (or night). His eyes were bloodshot behind his steamy Harry Potter glasses. I didn't get a chance to say much before Buffy hustled me down the hallway toward the next door, making me feel like a five-year-old on Halloween without any hope of treats. Or tricks, even.

"Do you know that guy?" Buffy asked after I heard Micah's door shut.

"Yeah, we go to the same school," I answered as neutrally as possible. *There's no need to mention we've known each other since third grade. Or that the last time*

I saw him I stuffed him under the stage just as the Green Zone thugs busted down the doors at the rave.

"Keep your distance. We don't want to associate with this *type* of people," she said with a sweeping gesture to the whole building or maybe the whole neighborhood.

"What type of people?" I asked all innocent. Inside I was seething. But I needed to play it cool. I didn't want any more time added to my community service sentence for being . . . myself.

"You know, TFC practically gave these places to the tenants to get them off the street and to stop causing trouble. Some of them," she said, lowering her voice to a whisper, "even came from that place where they found the bombs." She held on to her mobile tightly.

Buffy was talking about Micah and his mom and everyone else who'd lived in Black Dog Village, the homeless community in the salvage yard off Thirteenth Street. Someone had planted that evidence as an excuse to shut the place down. Clearly Buffy didn't know that.

I kept my trap shut and fantasized about taking Buffy around my neighborhood. If these squeaky clean "TFC projects," as she calls them, made her nervous, I can only imagine how the West End, with all its boarded-up houses and outright squats, would make her feel. That made *me* feel much better. For about a minute and a half.

We banged on a few more doors. Most people weren't home or didn't answer the door. An older gent took a flyer cautiously from my hand through the cracked door and mumbled a low thanks. He snapped the door shut almost before I could get my fingers out of the way. Locks locked and deadbolts bolted.

"Um, let's just slide them under the doors from now on," Buffy said nervously.

"He's harmless," I said and moved on to the next door. This place may not have eyeball scanners and Uzi-toting doormen like Buffy's used to, but it was clean and well lit and smelled of fresh paint and new carpet. I'm glad Micah and his mom got a decent place to live out of all this crap. I'd been kicking myself that he almost screwed it up by coming to my rave—or that I almost screwed it up for him by hosting the thing.

"Okay, tough girl, we've got a quota to meet." Buffy motioned me toward the next door.

Tough girl. That's what the Detention guy called me. *Yeah, I remember that.*

Who says you can't lie to TFC? Or leave out a few key details? Especially if they didn't ask. Which they didn't. They thought I was just some "tough girl" dating Spike, the lead singer of a crappy garage band with delusions of being the next Lo-Fi Strangers. My interrogator was way more interested in pinning something on the only adult at the rave: Rebecca Starr, aka Meme Girl. Detention guy figured I'd been duped into helping her. "You're just some dumb kid that she took advantage of," the guy in the black uniform said, his face creased in faux sympathy. "We know she's the brains of the operation, and you don't know anything about her subversive activities, do you, tough girl?"

I gave him my best oh-no-sir head shake.

They had no idea the rave was all my idea. Or that the point of it was to get out the word about the mandatory ID chips and how TFC was using them to brainwash us with false memories. And they certainly didn't know about Aiden and Winter's plan to wipe the chips clean with a little radio signal during the rave. They didn't hear it from my lips.

Someone famous once said, I've been seriously misunderestimated.

Let them underestimate you. *Book of Velvet*. Chapter 4, Verse 21. This verse was hard for me to follow all the time. Verse 22, though, not so much. They'll show their true colors soon enough—especially if you irritate the hell out of them.

I smiled to myself as we papered the rest of the floor with flyers.

"What the hell are you grinning at?" Buffy finally asked.

I didn't answer.

On the next floor, a little old lady told us to go to hell.

I'm thankful that I didn't look like myself. The lady was Mrs. Shaw. She and her husband owned Black Dog Salvage. She was friends with my boss, Mrs. Huxley, who owned the consignment shop, and with my mom.

"Ungrateful old biddy," Buffy hissed.

"You might not be so grateful if the city seized your business and home, and this was the only place you could find to live—that wasn't a squat," I told her, unable to keep it in any longer. Buffy didn't have a clue what a crap security score could do to someone. That's how Micah and his mom ended up in Black Dog Village in the first place. Or at least that's what my dad said.

"Let's just go. Mr. Mignon wants to talk to everyone anyway before the rally tomorrow," Buffy said as she headed toward the stairs.

The ride back to campaign headquarters was blissfully silent. I stared out the window while Buffy—whose real name is Trish McMillan—watched *Under the Dome* on her seat monitor. My screen cycled through a bunch of ads for the usual stuff. Starbucks. Glow hair tint. The Secrets' new album. TFC.

The Green Zone driver—our security for the "projects"—didn't crack a smile the whole trip. But I could hear his news feed.

. . . *the Coalition bombed targets in Norway, Greece, Portugal, and Saudi Arabia this week. The president says this newest jump in oil prices is only temporary. Patriot Party candidate Albert Mignon blames the president for the hike in food prices.*

My stomach grumbled at this. I checked my mobile and hoped fervently that Mignon was having pizza or doughnuts at this thing. I had barely enough credit to catch the bus home, if they hadn't raised the price again today. It was one of the mayor's brainwaves to tie bus fare to the price of gas. He claimed it was the only way the city could afford to keep public transportation going.

But there was no pizza. No doughnuts. Not even bottled water. Only Mayor Mignon in his glossy suit, with his equally glossy smile, waiting for us in the library.

He gave us his spiel on the importance of what we're doing for our country. Yada yada yada. And how his plan for mandatory ID programs across the country is just the thing to keep us all safe. He figures the chips help the police tell who belongs and who doesn't. I had to admit the guy has a certain slick charm. And he did make a weird kind of sense.

Still, pizza would've made me more of a believer. Or a less cranky agnostic.

But I know his ID chip does far more than tell the cops I'm not a Coalition terrorist.

The bus fare had gone up again. I flashed my mobile credit screen at the driver. "How far will this take me?"

"Not far," he muttered.

Story of my life.

Maybe there was a song in that.

MemeCast 2.1—
THE REBOOT

Okay, citizens. Meme Boy here. No, no, no. Let's reboot. NEO here. I am a hacker. And I'm not good at the political stuff like Meme Girl was, so I'm going to talk about what I know. Problem is, I know some useless crap.

Like this.

Back in the day, when the 'net was called the "electronic frontier," information roamed freely. People shared ideas, whether it was for code or cream puffs. And it was a Good Thing. But it hasn't been like that for a very, very long time. Maybe it never really was like that in the first place.

The 'net—or grid, as we like to call it now—is one centralized source of well-scrubbed (and monitored) information. It's fast, and we rely on it for everything. School. Work. Money. Security. We learn the things the grid-keepers want us to know. In turn, they watch our money and keep track of who they consider safe. Good deal, huh?

But it's a great big challenge for us white-hat hackers and skids and wannabes. We think we can free the beast from the chains and let the information run free again.

But we can't. Sure, we pry open a lock here and there. But then the grid-keepers lock it down stronger than before—and even offer us jobs to help them keep the information beast safe—from others like us.

So what can we do, citizens? Well, maybe it's time to build our own "electronic frontier." Something that's really open and not owned by anyone.

A few of us have already gotten started. Are you in?

We'll talk more later.

In the news, oil prices are up—all over. Not just here, like you heard on Action News. Europe, Asia, Africa. And that means everything else—like food—is going up because, well, you need oil to ship (and/or make) everything.

The Patriot Party now has someone running in nearly every major race in the country, including, of course, our Mayor Mignon running for Congress. My sources say that the Patriot Party is advertising heavily in Europe now, too. They've even had rallies outside Oslo and Athens.

By the way, my news sources aren't as extensive as Meme Girl's, so bear with me. If you've got news and are already online with us, IM me at Neo101.

Now, let's listen to a local band, the Wannabes, with their cover of Bob Marley's "Get Up, Stand Up."

BREAKING OUT OF WHATEVER

WINTER NOMURA

The tiny wings fluttered just as I'd imagined they would. I waved my hand over the prototype, and the thumb-sized rectangles of translucent plastic followed. And the closer I got to the surface, the more rapidly each plastic "wing" beat up and down.

The sound was just like the now-still hummingbirds inside my head.

The real sculpture could be massive. I surveyed my garden from the low table in the pagoda. There wasn't much space left between the crisscrossing walks for another kinetic sculpture, and I didn't want to crowd the ones already there. Each piece interacted with the next one like one big Rube Goldberg machine. But I could line the smooth bamboo fence with this piece. As you walked by it, a ripple of hummingbird wings would follow you—like thoughts chasing—

"If it smells like chicken, you're doing it wrong." Lina's voice brought my thoughts back down to earth. Through the open door, I could see Lina and my cousin, Aiden, in my workshop. His head was bent over a circuit board on my workbench.

"Don't make me laugh, or you will smell chicken," Aiden said. He steadied the soldering iron in his right hand and, with his left, carefully fed a small bit of the soldering wire into the joint between the component and track on the board. He touched it with the tip of the iron to join the two. At least that's what was supposed to happen.

Lina peered over his shoulder and then mimed strangling him behind his back. The boy could crack code and schmooze people with the best of them, but his DIY skills needed some serious work. He was a breaker, not a maker, at heart. I'd tried to teach him to solder, but Lina was way more patient than me. She stroked her lip ring thoughtfully as she watched Aiden work.

She glanced up and caught me looking at her. I blushed, but she just smiled. I was such a newbie at this romance thing.

"The joint is supposed to look like a tiny little volcano," Lina said calmly, turning her attention back to Aiden.

Apparently it did not. Aiden tossed the board onto the

table. I could see a blob of flux on the PCB from here.

"We could use solderless breadboard or printed circuits," Aiden protested.

He had a point. A breadboard or printed circuit might have been easier, but these units needed to be sturdy. The little white boxes might go anywhere—outside, in attics, wherever.

Lina stole a glance at me over her delightfully nerdy black glasses and then sighed dramatically. "You wanted to help."

They were building routers for our new network. We'd moved up a level of defunct, old-school tech—from radios to ad hoc Wi-Fi networks. Very 2012. Aiden had hacked together some rather genius code to make the software work, and now he wanted to learn more of the hardware side. Lina and I could make the nodes much faster—alone—but you can't learn if you don't do.

The MemeNet—and Lina with all her little projects—had taken over my workshop.

She rifled through the other crap on the workbench until she found what she was looking for. "Time to learn desoldering," Lina said with a certain amount of earnest glee as she brandished a copper desoldering braid at Aiden. She winked at me.

Lina had kind of taken over my heart the same way she'd taken over my workshop.

We met in the park—over an old 64-bit game console. We'd both reached for it at Sun Yu's stall, and I found myself looking up at that lip ring of hers. (She is several inches taller than me.) I let her have the PlayStation, and she traded Yu an oscilloscope for it. Lina and Big Steven were bartering what they'd salvaged from their workshop in the Rocket Garden. (That's what they called the old transportation museum scrapyard; it was full of rocket parts and other museum castoffs.) They'd narrowly escaped getting picked up at the rave themselves. Steven figured they'd better move their gear out of the old junkyard in case someone talked.

Lina's hair had been pink and long that day. You could see the dirty blond streaks underneath the phosphorescent color. Now her hair was short and dark, which made her steel blue eyes sparkle through behind her glasses. And the lip ring . . . well, it was hot.

That day I traded her an old payphone for a hoodie she'd made that shut off screens when you zipped it all the way up. She'd sewn a fabruino microcontroller that blocked mobile signals into an embroidered patch and ran the circuit through the threads and the metal zipper. She'd said, with that earnest glee in her eye, that she could program the sweatshirt to block any kind of signal. I invited her and Steven to move the maker space to my workshop right then and there. If it was okay with Grandfather, I hastily added, since I wasn't technically living here anymore. I'd moved back in with my parents in the Tamarind Bay compound.

And now Lina was here almost every day helping us

make nodes for the new network—the MemeNet, Aiden dubbed it—while Steven, Micah, and Nora helped spread the little plastic boxes throughout the city.

Nora James breezed in through the back gate. We'd given her the code after the rave. With her pink top, green shorts, sandals, and glossy hair, she looked like the daughter my mom would love to shop for. I was wearing torn jeans and a black T-shirt with a circuitry pattern Lina had embroidered in red. This fabruino microcircuit monitored the heartbeat and respiration of the wearer—and transmitted the results to a mobile. A girlfriend lie detector shirt, Lina called it.

I'd blushed when she'd said the g-word.

"Ready for school?" Nora asked.

I groaned. It started tomorrow. Mom already had my school uniforms laid out—and fully accessorized, within the dress code of Tamarind Day School.

"Me neither." Nora distractedly pulled the sweaty strands of her hair into a stubby ponytail and fastened it with a rubber band. She'd probably taken the bus and/ or walked from her mother's apartment downtown. She slummed it on the weekends now that her parents were separated.

"I thought you loved school, miss prep and all that." I watched her stare off in the direction of the workshop.

Nora had been part of the popular crowd all her life. Whereas Micah, Velvet, and I ate at the so-called freaks-and-geeks table. Not that I'd trade places. But I wondered how she and Micah had become an item. And it mystified me how she and I had become friends. Oh, I'd heard the *how* part many times, but it was like one of those stories your parents tell you about something you did when you were three but you have no memory of it whatsoever. Mine loved to recite how I barfed up oysters on the waitress at the fancy restaurant. I didn't remember it, but I knew it was true. I still wanted to hurl every time I saw those slimly bundles of snot sitting on their half shells.

"I've never been the new girl before," Nora said quietly. Her prep girl façade fell away, and I could see her thoughts, her fears, flashing across her face, however briefly. I wasn't convinced she was really worried about school, but that didn't matter. In that instant, I could believe we were friends.

"I'm not going to lie. It sucks." I'd changed schools a few times in my life, and at Homeland High No. 17 I'd finally found friends I could stand. A skateboarding artist, a songwriting thrift-store diva, and a few wannabe garage band heroes. And now a gutsy prep. "You'll be fine," I told her.

I wasn't so sure about me. Or Lina.

Lina's school, the artsy, progressive one by the university, had been closed down because they refused to check students (and staff) for the new mandatory ID chip—which Lina didn't have. Neither did her folks, who taught there at Community High. The Walshes were officially off-grid now, which meant Lina would have to be homeschooled or something.

"Thanks," Nora said with a laugh. "Got the book?"

I motioned for her to follow me into the workshop. The old garage was just big enough for a sizeable workbench, a few tables, and several mismatched shelves of equipment and junk. One table was stacked with routers, computer parts, and antennae. Another was covered with baggies filled with Lina's newest kit idea, and along the far wall were boxes of radios.

Aiden attempted to say hi, but his taskmaster cracked her copper whip. "Finish that contact point first—or this hotspot will be toast." Lina laughed at her own awful joke.

Nora laughed, too. "What are these?" she asked, distracted by the worktable strewn with baggies. Each contained wires, LEDs, small breadboards, and other bits.

I walked to the shelf and took down her book, which sat next to a Watchman lunchbox and another custom order. Some people had requested special hidey-holes for their pieces of the MemeNet, the underground network we were building.

"DIY kits," Lina answered while scrutinizing Aiden's work.

"Lina sells them down in the park," Aiden explained now that he was free to talk. "You can make your own blink light—without soldering," he added over his shoulder.

Lina's DIY kits included the type of breadboard onto which you just popped the diodes and lights in place, kind of like Legos. This microcontroller—popular years ago—made it easy for anybody to build and program their own hardware.

"Why would anyone want to do that?" Nora asked, holding one of the baggies like it had dog poop inside.

"To learn how to do it," Lina and I answered together.

"And then you can come up with something cool of your own," Lina added. "I show you how to make a dumb blinking light, and you turn around and make an alarm clock or a radio or a router."

"But I can buy an alarm clock," Nora said.

"You know, Leens, you should have a forum on our network where people can post mods and instructions," I said to Lina.

"And requests," Lina added excitedly. I could see the possibilities darting through her brain.

I rummaged around the workspace to find something to write on, and Lina and I started ticking off ideas to each other. She scribbled them down. I caught a whiff of her mom's homemade lavender soap as Lina leaned closer.

Nora cleared her throat. She'd obviously said something that I didn't catch. Mr. Explainer was trying to tell her about open source hardware and programmable microcontrollers, but Nora cut him off. "Whatever," Nora said. "Why do you guys want to build or hack everything yourself?"

The three of us exchanged blank looks.

"I don't understand the question," I said finally.

"Why not?" Aiden said, answering Nora.

Nora laughed. "I get why *you* hack," she said to Aiden. "Sort of. It's the thrill to break into something, right?"

Aiden shrugged. I knew it went deeper than that for him. He had this whole thing about the Universe prodding him along to open doors that needed opening. Or something like that. He hadn't mentioned it much lately.

"That's just one part of hacking," I said. "It's how you put it back together. That router is a hack. This T-shirt. My art. That book. All beautiful hacks."

Lina looked thoughtful for a second. "A hacker isn't just someone who breaks *into* something," she said to Nora. "She's someone who breaks *out* of something."

Aiden let out a low whistle with only the faintest hint of mockery on his face.

Nora shook her head. "Breaks out of what?" She had that exasperated look Mom gets when I express zero interest in clothes—or boys.

"Of whatever," Lina answered seriously. She threw up her arms to take in life, the universe, and everything.

My heart beat like the wings of a hummingbird.

Lina eyeballed me mischievously as her mobile vibrated in her pocket. *This girlfriend shirt might have to mysteriously disappear in the laundry when I get home.*

4.0

NOTHING HAPPENING HERE

VELVET

Crap. I couldn't even escape him on the bus. There he was, blathering away on the newscast that rolled across the seat in front of me. Mayor Mignon. Now he was blaming the Coalition for the high price of oil and warning citizens that things were only going to get worse—unless we did something about it. *We have the right to take extraordinary actions to preserve our way of life. We're on the right track,* yada yada yada, *but we might need to make certain sacrifices.*

Sacrifices? You didn't see *him* making any sacrifices. He'd pulled away from school in a gas-guzzling armored Bradley, no doubt going to his comfy home in some high-priced, high-security compound.

I pulled out my little leather notebook from my bag

and tried to noodle around with a song idea. I didn't get very far. Lyrically or physically.

A TFC ad scrolled across the screen. A beautiful but worried woman stepped out of a meeting. She pressed the TFC icon on her Nomura mobile and spoke into the phone. When she hung up, a calm look spread across her face and she strode back into the meeting. The ad ended with the typical blue-skies-green-pastures TFC scene with "Forget your cares anywhere, anytime" spelled out across the fluffy clouds. *App coming to Hakita mobiles October 1* trailed lazily across the bottom of the screen.

The bus dropped me off at Market Street. It was still six blocks to the pedestrian bridge over the freeway and another three blocks through the West End to my house. My feet already felt like planks of wood from canvassing all day.

Mayor Mignon has your best interests at heart.

Crap on a stick.

I jammed in my earbuds and cranked up a music 'cast on my mobile in a vain attempt to drown out those weird thoughts. The Lo-Fi's were playing "Boom!" I walked for four or five blocks listening to the pounding beat.

. . . all your crooked pictures . . .

As I rounded the corner onto Market Street, the song crescendoed a bit louder than I remembered, and I felt the ground tremble. I pulled out my earbuds just in time to hear sirens and screams—and see smoke belching from a building less than a block away. A few minutes later and I would've been right in front of ground zero.

Cop cars ringed the smoking hole that was once TFC No. 23.

The street was littered with glittering shards of glass and oddly shaped boxes.

One cop in a gas mask directed me to stay back. She pulled off the mask and threw it to the ground. She wiped her eyes on her sleeve before screaming something in my general direction. Another cop dragged out a bloodied kid maybe six or seven years old. He was kicking and screaming, and as soon as the cop stupidly set him down, he dashed back toward the building. The cop caught hold of the kid's lime green T-shirt and the belt loop of his khaki shorts and reeled him back into a tight bear hug. The kid sagged into the cop's arms and let himself be carried to the waiting ambulance.

My wooden feet were rooted into the asphalt.

Something about the scene—other than the obvious death and destruction—bothered me, but I couldn't think what it was. I couldn't think of anything except that kid in the lime T-shirt.

The woman cop screamed something again, and I realized she was talking to me. "Go already," she said, finally, in a broken sob.

It took every ounce of willpower to rip my feet from the ground and back away from the scene, but not before I put my sneaker through a cardboard coffin. I tried to shake the thing off my foot, but it clung to me as ash began to fall like hot, sticky snowflakes. I clawed the cardboard away with my hands, panic rising in my gut.

The name on the coffin was VELVET K.

Run. *Book of Velvet*. Some fucking chapter and verse. Run.

I ran until my feet turned into splinters.

Forget your cares, said a voice in my head.

THE BIRTH OF A NOT-SO-BRILLIANT IDEA

NORA JAMES

My mood was so not glossy. Lina had given me a headache. I broke a nail lugging my suitcase into the tacky old elevator. The book I'd picked up from Winter, which was rolled up in my Halstead jeans, wasn't helping either. And the thought of Mom living alone in this place still made me uneasy. No security other than old-fashioned locks, and as Mom always points out, neighbors who give a damn. The elevator actually had buttons, and it shimmied as it descended the few floors between our apartment and Mom's office on the ground floor.

The real problem, though, was that school started tomorrow, and I wasn't sure how I felt about going back to the compound. I'd told Winter that I was worried about being the new girl at Los Palamos High, but that wasn't it.

Three months ago, I was ecstatic at the thought of moving to LP. But then school ended in a haze, and I found myself at the beach with Mom. No Dad. He'd moved to the compound without us. Mom then told me this crazy story, which was so not me. Or so I thought. At the time, I was sure she'd concocted it to turn me against Dad. She said he beat her—like all the time—and that he'd even doped me so I'd forget. I just couldn't believe it.

So I called Dad to come get me.

The Los Palamos experience was not all that I'd imagined it to be.

The elevator shuddered to a halt. I pulled my luggage into the lobby, a term I use very loosely. Back in the day, this place was a hotel. Now the restaurant and bar were all boarded up. Who'd really want to eat here, anyway? But there were a couple of offices on the first floor. A massage therapist. Spiritual medium. Alcoholics Anonymous. And the law offices of Sidney Woolf James, Esquire.

Mom got the best space, at least. Two whole rooms. I deposited my stuff in the tiny waiting room outside her actual office. I could see through the frosted glass door that she still had a client. Like everything in the apartment, the office reminded me of our town house in Arlington Heights. Everything here came from there: the dining room chairs, the fake plants, the glossy architectural magazines, and even the historic-trust sage paint on the accent wall. Mom's laugh cut through the thin walls.

Really, this place was not so bad.

Mom's mobile warbled out a familiar tune. Dad. It must be almost five. At the official end of every weekend this summer, he'd called to make sure I was on my way home.

Have to go soon, I texted Micah. He should have been here by now.

One of Mom's clients, that newscaster who'd gotten fired and now rehired at Action News, opened the office door. She stopped and looked at me as if trying to place me. Or maybe she was deciding whether to let me in on something. Then, shaking her head the tiniest bit, she flashed a glossy smile at me and moved on.

I felt like I should know her. I mean, I knew who she was. Rebecca Starr, the Action News reporter. She covered Micah, Winter, and me putting out the underground comic, *Memento.* Mom showed me a bootleg copy of the video where Ms. Starr interviewed me just as I was being taken away to Detention. It was still hard to believe it was me, but there I was, telling the world how my father's own company was the one blowing up cars and blaming it on Coalition terrorists. I don't remember any of it, of course.

My mobile vibrated. *Sorry. Ran into trouble. Explain later. M. BTW, saw V.* I snapped it shut without replying.

"Mom? I'm ready." I stepped into her office, but she was staring at her mobile. "What is it?"

She stuffed the mobile into her jeans pocket before walking slowly over to me. "Your father is suing for sole custody."

It felt like someone had sucked all the air out of the stuffy little office—and me. I put a hand on a hard-backed dining room chair Mom used for clients. Mom reached for me, but I pulled away. And I felt even worse because I had.

"It'll be okay, Nora," she murmured.

"What does that mean? Would I ever see you?" I know I had questioned whether Mom was trying to take me away from Dad, but she'd been right about him—and I couldn't imagine not seeing her.

And she's my mom.

"That depends on the court." She sounded far away.

"He can't do that," I stammered stupidly. I knew he could do whatever he damn well liked. Ethan Trevor James III, CEO of Green Zone, is used to getting his way.

"Don't worry, hon. I'll fight it." Mom snapped back to the here and now. "Has he ever raised his voice to you or . . ." Mom trailed off.

I shook my head, but there had been times when I could see he was very close to losing it. And it kind of scared me. Like the time I came home late from a date with Tom. (This was before Micah and I rediscovered each other at the rave.) Dad was pissed in more ways than one and nearly threw a beer bottle at me. He apologized profusely and even bought me a new charm—a tiny silver tiara—for my bracelet. I didn't tell Mom this, though.

"Now I wish I could prove that he, you know," Mom said glumly.

She'd erased almost every memory of abuse with a little white pill at her favorite TFC, number 23. She only learned about what Dad had been doing to her (and she to herself) when she heard my confession in Detention—right before I got the big pill of forgetting. Then she told me the whole crazy story. It had been particularly hard for me to believe the part about Dad—until I saw his eyes as he held that beer bottle. He wouldn't hurt me, I told myself, but I still locked my bedroom door that night.

It was also hard for me to believe that Mom put up with the abuse. But this Mom sitting before me was a far cry from the one I remember from the last six or seven years of my life. This Sidney James left Dad, started up her old law practice defending the "undefendable" (Dad's words), and generally kicked butt. And this was the Mom I remember from when I was little. Would she have been this person all along if she hadn't made so many trips to TFC No. 23 to forget her cares? *They* certainly knew the truth.

"Too bad you can't get your records from TFC," I said as I dragged my bags out the main door.

Mom stopped and stared at me as if I'd said something brilliant.

"Mom, I was kidding." I stumbled on the sidewalk, but she caught me.

"I am a lawyer." She grinned as she took my bags from me and threw them in the back of the car Dad had sent to take me "home." The driver didn't (wouldn't) even get out of the car in *this* neighborhood.

A familiar sound rumbled from the next block, and I saw a plume of smoke rising over the 24-hour pharmacy down the street. Funny, the new ID program hadn't improved security in this neighborhood.

Mom suddenly turned serious again and shoved me into the car. The driver already had the engine running, and the Kevlan was sliding over the back windows.

"Some people will stop at nothing to get their way," I heard Mom mutter as she shut my car door.

I wondered if some people included Dad.

6.0

LITTLE BOXES ON THE HILLSIDE

NORA

I held my breath as the limo passed through the new gate scanner into the Los Palamos compound. The big, movie-star-looking iron gate swung open slowly, and the driver sped through, nearly scraping the sides of the Bradley. Inside the gates, the seat screen shifted mid-ad from Home Security Depot to the Glam Rapid Clear Facial at LP Aesthetics.

We passed by rows upon rows of neatly trimmed lawns with nearly identical stucco houses and a car in every garage. Sometimes you could catch a glimmer of rippling blue-green in the backyards. The compound was laid out like a wagon wheel. Palm trees swayed along the main spoke, Palomino Way. It led to Rodeo Drive, which ringed the center shopping plaza, the Galleria.

The whole compound was supposed to look like Southern California—instead of Northern Virginia.

I'd really been looking forward to living the *Behind the Gates* lifestyle in Los Palamos. The houses. The shopping. The boys.

When we first rolled through those gates, that first day after Dad picked me up from the beach, Los Palamos was as glossy as I'd expected it. Dad played tour guide, and I was loving it. All the gray and cream and yellow houses, each little neighborhood more glossy than the next. The houses got bigger and the lots smaller as we cut across the spokes of the wheel. Then we turned into a neighborhood with big houses perched on little hills.

"Where's ours?" I asked. Our ancient town house in Arlington Heights had been Mom's dream home. Tiny rooms with exposed brick and hardwood floors, all lovingly restored and painted in historically accurate colors. A real piece of the past, she'd called it. I'd always thought the past should stay dead and buried. Or, at a bare minimum, have bigger closets and a pool.

Dad slowed down in front of an enormous place with cream stucco and a red tile roof. It was just like I'd pictured it. *My* dream house. I imagined a huge bedroom, a closet the size of the Gap, and my own bathroom.

"That's the Slayton's house now," he said through clenched teeth. Tom Slayton was the yearbook editor at my old school. I vaguely remembered a party at his place before finals, but that was at some big high-security building downtown.

Dad pulled away from the Slayton's curb and turned right onto Palomino Way. He kept going until we were back at the compound center. He pulled into the garage entrance of one of the high-rises. He didn't say anything until we stepped off the elevator on the ninth floor. Dad ret-scanned us into 901.

The place was about the size of our town house in Arlington Heights, but the apartment was almost bare. The only furniture Dad seemed to have bought was a big leather couch and a huge screen. The living room had floor-to-ceiling windows, but the view was of the next building.

"Mom said you'd gotten us a house." I turned on him.

He didn't look at me. He grabbed a beer from the fridge and then sank into the couch. "The Slaytons got the house. Rachael got some big promotion or something, and they were next on the list." He took a long drink of beer. I sat down on the other end of the couch. "The compound board 'did me a favor' and rented me this place until the investigation blows over."

Dad looked at me then, and it made me really uncomfortable for some reason.

"Investigation?" I searched my memory. Mom had mentioned something about an investigation, but I must not have been listening.

"Nothing to worry about, Princess." He smiled at me,

finally all Dad-like again. "Why don't you get settled in your room, and we'll order in for dinner? The building at least has room service." He flicked on a baseball game and took another long sip of beer.

That was three months ago. That was before he became CEO of Green Zone and we moved again. Before I found out why Dad's company was really under investigation.

The limo dropped me off in front of the Galleria Tower. The doorman took my bags to the elevator for me, and I said the word *penthouse*. The elevator scanned me in and smoothly lifted twenty-seven floors without even a quiver. Dad had been much happier since the "investigation" blew over, and Soft Target magically became his new company, Green Zone. I didn't get that part. He explained that Soft Target had declared bankruptcy, and then he'd reorganized everything to become the new company, Green Zone. Everything remained the same, but on paper the company under investigation no longer existed. I still didn't get it. The same people were involved. But it was good enough for compound board, and they fell all over themselves to give us the penthouse.

"When your mother comes to her senses," Dad had told me when we moved up those eighteen floors, "I'll push for a house. One that'll make the Slayton's look like a cardboard box."

The penthouse had its perks: a view of the compound, maid service, meals. And it was so big, an entire floor.

Half the time I couldn't tell if Dad was home or not. It felt like I had the whole place to myself. I enjoyed the illusion of it being all mine. Up to a point. But today I wanted some answers.

The lights flickered on when I stepped off the elevator into our apartment. It was so quiet I could hear the thrum of the air-conditioning.

Maybe I need a cat.

I checked Dad's room and his study, where he spent most of his time when he was home. No Dad.

The note in the kitchen said: "I'll try to be home for dinner, Princess." I'd seen that note a lot, and most of the time I ate alone.

I sank into my plush bed and contemplated the pale pink walls. The dark wood of the big, chunky furniture still looked very glossy against my favorite color. Everything was so much more grown-up (and spacious) than my little girly room in the town house. When I'd first seen my new bedroom, I felt like Dad really "got" me.

I could still hear the AC.

Bored already, I typed on my mobile and clicked send.

Micah replied immediately. *Sorry, make it up 2 U Sat?*

Micah was not big with the words, but it made me feel better.

I turned on a 'cast, the new one, *Under the Dome*, about the super-swank, super-max compound in Manhattan. Then I dumped my suitcase on my bed. I could just toss all the clothes in the hamper; the maid would do them tomorrow. Another perk. Besides, I had a ton of clothes in the closet for school tomorrow. Dad had gone overboard on the credit. I picked up my jeans, and a book rolled out.

I scrambled to grab it, just in case Dad walked in. It was the book I'd gotten at Winter's. I'd met the Nomuras when they'd rescued Micah and me from that rave/concert thing. Winter and Aiden (and their families) explained what was going on. They'd confirmed the story Mom had told me, about Micah, Winter, and me putting out a comic and then getting our memories wiped. It was strange to find out I had this secret life I couldn't remember.

But when I'd seen Micah at the rave, something clicked.

It was like we had known each other in another life.

And I couldn't deny Mom's story—about me, at least—any longer.

And now I was bringing my secret life home, which was dangerous territory. I'd agreed to take a node back to Los Palamos. The idea of having one twenty-seven floors up in the center of the biggest compound in Hamilton made both Nomura cousins ridiculously happy. I said I'd take one, but I hadn't really decided if I'd actually turn it on. What if Dad found it? His company supposedly ran Detention (and worse) for TFC.

"Nora?" Dad, the king of timing, called from the kitchen. I could hear the rustling of plastic and the clink of bottles.

"Coming!" I tucked the book under my pillows and stuffed my clothes into the hamper in my bathroom.

In the kitchen, Dad was opening take-out containers and arranging them like a buffet on the table. He had a football game on mute on the small screen over the counter. The ticker across the bottom said something about a Middle East government falling to the Coalition. The kitchen smelled like hot chilis and ginger and garlic. I slid into my seat. A bouquet of yellow carnations with a sprig of baby's breath lay across my plate. I poked my nose in the containers, suddenly ravenous. Kung Pao shrimp. Sesame chicken. Crispy beef. Won Ton soup. He'd gotten all my favorites.

"I'm so glad you're home, Princess." He beamed at me, all Dad-like. He poured me a soda and opened himself a beer. He even put the flowers in a vase for me.

We passed around take-out boxes, chit-chatted about school and if I had everything I needed. He reminded me—again—what a great school Los Palamos High is (much better than Homeland High No. 17) and how it'll look great on college apps. Then we fell into an at-first comfortable silence as we chewed. All the while, though, I was trying to work up the courage to ask him what I really wanted to know.

He beat me to it.

"Your mother probably told you what's going on," Dad finally said.

I nodded while I crunched a mouthful of crispy beef. I

washed it down with Diet Coke, breathed in, and pushed away my plate. "Dad, why don't you want me to see Mom?"

He took a sip of his beer before answering.

"Princess." He sounded exactly like he had when he'd explained what happened to my goldfish when I was five and had fed it the sink cleaner instead of fish food. "Your mother is going through some changes right now. I'm not mad that she suddenly left me with no warning." He pushed away his plate, too. "She's got to work out whatever it is herself. But she's living in a dangerous part of town and working with equally dangerous people. You shouldn't be exposed to that."

"Her place isn't so bad," I said lamely. Dad had a talent for turning everything around and making whatever I'd planned to say seem silly or meaningless.

"A bomb went off near her place today, Nora. She can't protect you, and she can't afford to take care of you like I can." He made a small look-at-all-this gesture. "And I can give you the finest education and the tightest security money can buy. And you'll meet the right people here. I've got your best interests at heart, Princess." His smile was so full of Dadness that I almost felt bad for asking the question. Almost.

He tucked his mobile into his pocket and leaned in to kiss me on the forehead. "And no judge is going to see it any differently," he whispered. His warm Dad voice became as cool as a knife. "I've got some work to do." He disappeared into his study.

With a chill, I realized Dad was so right. His case was much stronger than Mom's. (He should have been the lawyer.) Mom had left him and taken me with her. And the only proof that he mistreated Mom was in the records of TFC. And Green Zone, his company, was the security arm of that company.

Even if she got the records, who knows what they'd say when he was done with them. But was he really that kind of guy? According to the Nomuras (and Mom), he was. And I knew Dad's former company was guilty of setting off car bombs around the city to scare people. Micah and I had put that in *Memento*.

No matter how much I've been told what I did (or what Dad did), it seems like *that* Nora was another person. And so was *that* Dad.

My appetite evaporated. I put the take-out containers in the fridge and went back to my room.

I sat on my bed again for about half a second before pulling out the book from under the pillows. I'd given this book to Winter and Aiden to use for a reason. It was my old world history textbook from Homeland High. I cracked it open to the chapter on the Renaissance. They'd neatly hollowed out the center of the book to hide their network node, or hotspot, or whatever they were calling it. (It was this shiny white plastic box with a nub of antennae.) But they'd carefully left the chapter title—and the words I'd written across the top:

YOUR FATHER BEATS YOUR MOTHER.

I'd written it there before going to the Big D—none of which I remembered, of course. After I'd discovered it in a box at Mom's new apartment, I'd pull the book out every once in a while to remind myself I wasn't crazy. (And that Mom wasn't, either.)

Suddenly, I understood what Lina meant about breaking out. Of whatever.

I flicked the power switch on, closed up the book, and set it on a high shelf near the window.

My pocket vibrated. I pulled out the new mobile Aiden had given me. He was calling this model the Nomura Freedom. It looked just like the Chipster, but the Freedom only connected to the new underground network they were building.

The message said, "Welcome to the MemeNet."

7.0

IF IT AIN'T BAROQUE

AIDEN NOMURA

The code streaming across my screen was so rococo, so encrusted with the software equivalent of gold leaf and curlicues, that it was amazing the monstrosity ran at all. It should just collapse under its own committee-designed, security-bloated weight. All the programmers at TFC and Soft Target (and Green Zone, or whatever they called themselves now) must have had their fingers in this code.

The universe muttered something clever as I clicked on a particularly elephantine loop and found the open door I was looking for. My father peered over my shoulder.

"That's how we can add records to the database," I said, pointing to the query string. "We just need to figure out how to call the real database." We only had access to the development one, which was on one of TFC's less secure servers.

"You know, Ichiro, I never dreamed I'd be making fake IDs when you hired me twenty years ago," Aunt Spring said as she sipped her coffee.

The Nomura CEO (aka my father) and its chief hardware designer (Winter's mother) were hovering behind my workstation in the testing lab. Since my former "mentor" Roger had bailed on us, it had become my office and ground zero for my "internship" activities.

Dad arched an eyebrow at her. "That's what we have Aiden for," he added with a thin smile. He'd grudgingly come to appreciate my hacking skills this summer. He ran his fingers through his hair as he pondered the screen. The hair thing was one of his tells. To the world he presented this unflappable, all business exterior. But he was worried.

My aunt crossed the arms of her perfectly pressed navy suit and said nothing.

"I think the hack will work, but it's not going to be bulletproof—or even armor-plated," I explained as I scrolled through the database code on screen for them. Hackers thought of code in terms of its lossage resistance, or how tight it was. Bulletproof and armor-plated were the highest levels, and that kind of code could survive anything thrown at it. Mine, not so much. "In fact, it might be fairly brittle," I confessed. TFC could change their code at anytime, and we'd be screwed.

"What does that mean in non-hackish?" Aunt Spring asked. A trace of distaste crept into her voice. She was a very by-the-book engineer.

I didn't take the jab personally. Winter said her folks were still struggling to grasp what had happened to them.

Nomura Electronics had developed Hamilton's mandatory ID chip for TFC in the first place. Under duress, though. Aunt Spring and Uncle Brian had designed the chip, and then when Dad balked at delivering it to TFC, the company had Winter's parents snatched and thrown into Detention (which is run by TFC and its minions) until the product was ready to ship. Then TFC wiped their brains and sent them on their merry way—with the new chips and a few fake memories of living in Japan stuffed in their wetware. Earlier this summer, Winter and I figured out how to erase the implanted memories, leaving her parents with a big gaping hole in their lives. So my aunt was understandably cranky.

"He means it's not going to be pretty and might break at any moment," Dad said patiently.

"Maybe we should just stick to the first part of the plan," Spring said. Her heels brought her almost up to Dad's eye level. "Until we get this part sorted out." She waved her coffee cup in the general direction of my screen.

Dad ran his hand through his hair again and nodded.

The plan had been simple. Replace the mandatory ID chip Mignon and his TFC cohorts had forced on the good citizens of Hamilton with one that didn't brainwash people with fake memories and whatever. It should be cake. Spring still had the designs for the chip. She and Uncle Brian just had to neuter the chip so that TFC couldn't control it—or detect the swap. Okay, maybe not so cake.

However, after spending much of August on the chip and its software, we'd realized a glaring flaw in our plan. The obviosity of it had been stunning. We could easily copy and beam the data from one chip to another. This helped the users who already had the ID chip but just wanted to avoid all that fake-memory, brainwashing crap. But what about those people who didn't have the chip in the first place? Their data wasn't in the city's database. We could put in our own glossy new chips, but once the cops scanned them, they'd find out instantly the wearer wasn't registered—and that the ID was fake. Hello, Detention. For all of us.

That's where I came in. The hack in question was to be able to add people to the official database. Thanks to Roger, we still had backdoor access to the development database for the ID chip. That's the one the programmers use when writing and testing the software that talks to the chip. The development database was nothing but dummy data, but it was set up exactly like the real production database.

I whipped out my mobile and showed Dad and Spring how we could add names remotely. I scanned the test chip Aunt Spring had brought and then entered some fake info. Fred Barney. 123 Bedrock Way. I tapped a social security number. Fred's data populated the development database I'd pulled up on another screen.

"Nice job," Aunt Spring said.

"It works—on the *development* database," I reminded them. "I still need to figure out how to access the real one, wherever it is."

"You'll figure it out," Dad said, turning to leave.

It was reassuring that he actually believed it. Aunt Spring didn't look so sure. But that wasn't what was worrying me.

"Dad, what if the link breaks or TFC changes something after we give them to people? They could get arrested." Or worse. And it could all get traced back to us. I ran my hand through my hair. I didn't know if I could take that responsibility.

Dad put his hand on my shoulder. "I know. Let me worry about that."

Dad and Spring agreed that we'd start handing out replacement chips as soon as possible while I worked on phase two. "We need to undo the damage we've done before Hakita takes over," Dad commented to no one in particular. He'd told me that Hakita Electronics had recently inked a deal with TFC to offer the same TFC applications on their phones. That probably meant TFC was replacing us, and we might lose all access to future chip and software designs. The New TFC ad was already hawking Hakita rather than Nomura mobiles.

"It might take some nefarious social engineering to get database access," I said. I'd have to do some cold calling and/or digital dumpster diving. Then maybe I could use a security audit tool to crack the password. Maybe.

"This is your call, Ichiro. But you know what Gretchen would say," Aunt Spring said as she left the room. Dad stared after her. Gretchen, my mom, knew about some of my exploits, but she would not like me getting into any danger. Dad ran his hand through his hair one more time. He was definitely worried—about both of us. Mom was still in Zurich. Flights were getting fewer between here and Europe, and she still had business to wrap up. Some touchy deal with Riyad. Her bank was full of Saudi money.

"Be careful," he finally said as he made his exit. "Take Jao if you need to go anywhere." He paused at the door. "And if you get caught, tell them you're with Hakita." He cracked another thin smile.

Dad's lame attempt at humor didn't make me feel any better.

The universe murmured in agreement.

8.0

CHAPTER AND VERSE

MICAH

The rent-a-cop at the door was wanding everyone behind the ear—on top of the usual bag and body search. *No ID, No ENTRY*, the new sign said above the security station. And if you were dumb enough to show up without one of the new mandatory ID chips tucked into your skull, you wouldn't get a measly hour after school under the watchful eye of Coach Biggins. The real cop dozing in his car outside would cart you off to Detention. The Big D variety.

I sucked in a breath and dutifully submitted, the scanner chiming as the wand passed behind my right ear. Rent-a-cop number 2 patted me down and then poked around in my messenger bag. As he pulled out a large coffee-table book, I had another intense feeling of déjà vu. He eyeballed me as he read the cover: *Graphic Novels of the Twentieth Century*. The school library sticker was starting to come loose from the spine.

"I forgot to return it after exams," I said as nonchalantly as I could manage. My heart was racing.

He grunted at me and shoved the book back into my bag. I slung it over my shoulder and headed to my locker—and let out a huge breath.

The halls seemed quieter, emptier than I remember, like it was senior skip day or like the time half the school was out with bird flu. *Maybe this is what school looks like when you actually get here on time.*

The overhead lights flickered for a second before they settled back into their everyday, grating hum. The ad on my locker cycled from Guy Code Deodorant to Powerco Generators. *Somebody programming these things has a warped sense of humor.*

As I tried out the new thumbprint scan on the lockers, I spotted Velvet, her arms full of streamers, that same cheerleader girl who'd eyeballed me in my skimpy towel yesterday. Not my finest look, I know. Cheerleader chick bustled off with several Mignon minions in the direction of the gym. Red, white, and blue signs papered the hallway. Students for Mignon Rally. 3 p.m. today.

I'd rather go skinnydipping in a vat of hot French fry grease than listen to him. The man was a complete douche.

The first bell rang, and I dashed off to homeroom. No

skateboards in school this year. Mom made a major point of that this morning. Thou shalt not screw up our good thing. She didn't say it in so many words, but that's what she meant. We finally had a decent place to live.

Mom was so proud to have gotten us the apartment. I had to admit I almost cried when I saw the bathroom—with actual hot water—and my tiny little loft space with a real-person-sized bed. Black Dog Village had outdoor solar-heated showers, which was fine in the summer, but in the winter you'd freeze your nads off. So I used to grab a shower in the locker room before school and skate like hell to get to class on time—or not. Old habits.

I walked into Mrs. Eakins's homeroom, fully expecting not to get a seat. Usually every chair in every class was taken—and then some. I'd spent most of last year perpetually late and perpetually sitting on the floor against the back wall. This year there were desks to spare. Still, I took a seat in the back.

How many kids aren't here because of the chip thing? Maybe some moved to compounds or other schools. Nora and Winter (and her cousin Aiden) were going to school behind their gates in Los Palamos and Tamarind Bay. Except for Velvet, my little crew would be all guys this year. And I wasn't sure about V. Not that she wasn't a guy. No doubt about that. No, I wasn't sure she was one of us anymore. She'd seemed different to Aiden a few weeks ago when she'd showed up at his house campaigning for Mignon. She'd seemed different to me yesterday, too. It was almost like she'd been brainwashed into supporting the mayor. Had they done something more to her than a brain bleach and community service? Had they added some memories? Erased too many? Could we trust her? I didn't know. But she could've been putting on an act for the cheerleader chick or the Mignon people. I could hear her now: *Sometimes you can't let your freak flag fly too high, or someone will lop it the hell off. And give you more community service time. Book of Velvet.* I could imagine her spouting some shit like that. Still. A sign, a wink even, would've been nice.

While Mrs. Eakins called the roll, I pulled out my sketch pad and doodled coffins. Homeland Teen News droned on about security changes, dress codes, committees, and club signups. The obligatory TFC ad was followed by a Patriot Party one. Then the principal announced that the school, and parts of the downtown area, might be subject to rolling blackouts through the fall, at least until it cooled off. She didn't mention anything about the winter and heat. If a blackout happened during school, the principal said with a glossy smile on her face, then make your way calmly to the illuminated emergency exit.

Return your tray tables to the upright position and grab your seat cushion; it's going to be a bumpy ride, I thought.

We'd already been put on an energy meter in our new

apartment. If you went over your electricity ration, you'd get cut off for the day. Or until you paid an overage fee. Mom only let me run the AC a few hours a day—usually at night so we could sleep.

HTN didn't say anything about the protests I saw yesterday; neither did the Action News 'cast last night. Just something about another bombing. I wasn't really surprised, though I was shocked to see Rebecca Starr (aka Meme Girl) back on the air like all was forgiven. They must have brain bleached her, but she was looking hotter than ever.

I drew more coffins.

Between second and third periods, I ducked into the library. The usual librarian, Ms. Curtis, wasn't there. A sour-looking old guy glowered at me from the checkout counter as I headed toward the back of the library, to the old encyclopedia section. I'd figured no one used these anymore, and I was right. The dust was thick on the ancient set of *Encyclopedia Americana*'s. I pulled out M-Na and made a show of fumbling and dropping it accidentally. As I squatted to pick it up, my back blocking the security camera overhead, I pulled out the book from my messenger bag and shoved it under the bookcase. I hoped the thing worked under there. Inside the hollowed-out volume was a MemeNet hotspot. I'd turned it on during a quick pitstop in the second-floor bathroom stall after homeroom. As I rose, someone cleared his throat behind me.

"Can I help you with something, young man?" the librarian asked, the frost thick on his voice.

I slid the encyclopedia volume back into place. "Uh, no thanks. Just looking something up," I said quickly. The bell rang and I dashed away.

The rest of the morning just kind of trudged by. I saw Spike in Spanish and the other guys in history. We hadn't seen or spoken to one another much lately because everyone was on a short leash, legally speaking, for most of the summer. And that meant our mobiles were blocked, and technically we were supposed to be grounded, too. I got around that, sort of, because Mom worked nights—and I was used to dodging curfew. And Nora and I were using our aptly named Nomura Freedoms.

The guys seemed like the same old guys.

I added Velvet's name to one of my coffin doodles in English class. At least Winter and Nora were okay.

I missed Nora.

Winter, too, of course.

Finally, it was lunchtime. I was starving, as usual. Food pantry Pop-Tarts only last so long. I ordered two burgers, but the lunch lady said I was only entitled to one this year with my voucher (PKV—poor kid voucher—not its official name, though it should be). I could pay for it, she said. Or she could throw in some extra fries, she whispered conspiratorially when my stomach growled loudly.

I opted for the fries. The meat probably wasn't even real.

The new ad ticker running around the top of the walls, just below the cameras, said something about a hurricane and an oil spill off Tampa and a new government in Saudi Arabia. Then there was an ad for Hakita phones and the new TFC app.

I parked myself at our usual table toward the back. Spike was already chowing down. Richie and Steven joined us after a few minutes.

"This is going to be a real sausagefest," Richie declared as he slid into the seat opposite Spike. "Where the hell is Velvet, dude?"

The dude part was directed at Spike, who was now licking the fake burger juice from his fingers. He and Velvet had coupled up sometime between the end of school and the rave. A lot of that time was blank to me. But I'd also heard—from Winter—that Velvet been hanging out with Aiden at the same time. This year should be interesting. (Geez, we sound like an episode of *Camden's Creek* or *The Cul de Sac*.)

"Chill, she's helping with the rally." Spike started in on his fries.

"Shit," Steven grunted.

"It's her community service deal. We did ours, and we got off easy," Spike said.

"Yeah, I'd rather work the food bank any day," I said through a mouthful of burger. It was definitely not beef, but I didn't care. Mrs. B always said I ate like a stray dog, wolfing down everything because I didn't know where my next meal was coming from. Old habits.

Add Mrs. Brooks to that list of people I miss. She'd lived at Black Dog Village. In fact, she'd gotten Mom and me into BDV after we lost our apartment and were living out of our car.

"It's a good thing you weren't at the rave," Spike said, stealing one of my fries.

Huh? I stared at Spike and then the other guys for a second or two, but they didn't notice. I'd been there, and I'd talked to each of them before the show started.

"Yeah, you'd be doing community service until you were thirty-five," Richie added. He grimaced at the taste of his mystery-meat burrito.

"Or worse," Steven said without a trace of humor in his voice.

They didn't remember. Of course. I had been there. And I still felt incredibly douche-y for letting Velvet and the guys get picked up while Nora and I hid under the stage. Not that Velvet gave me much choice.

"What do you guys remember about that night?" I asked carefully.

Little Steven shrugged.

"Speak of the devil." Spike popped up as Velvet came toward us, balancing a tray on a box of flyers. Spike took the tray from her. She'd pulled a black hoodie, zipped up to her chin, over her yellow Mignon T-shirt. Only a sliver of it showed at her neck and waist. With her black skirt, tights, and boots, she looked like normal Velvet. A very warm Velvet. It was September. In Virginia. A tiny bead of perspiration was making its way down her forehead.

She dropped the box of flyers to the floor next to the table before she parked her butt into the chair opposite me. Her tray clattered against the table, spilling her fries, which Spike dutifully cleaned up.

"Kill me now," she said with a deep sigh. "Or better yet, off Buffy McCheerleader for me."

I knew then and there that I could erase her name from the coffin I'd doodled in English class.

I'd worried Detention had changed her, that they might have snipped a memory that made Velvet Velvet. And I worried they'd done the same thing to me.

But Velvet was all there. Chapter and verse.

Spike, on the other hand, I wasn't so sure of. He was seriously trying to feed Velvet a French fry. Dude.

WHEN THE LIGHTS GO OUT

VELVET

I waved off Spike's attempt to stuff my face with a soggy, crinkle-cut, cafeteria-issue fry.

Do not force-feed me. Anything. Food. Ideas. Whatever. *Book of Velvet*. Chapter 27, Verse 3. Unless, of course, you want your fingers bitten.

"Where the hell have you been?" Micah asked in mock irritation. The grin gave him away. Besides, he knew damn well where I'd been.

"Doing my time." I stuffed the burger into my mouth. It tasted like feet. Mom's community gardening efforts had finally paid off, and I'd lost my taste for crap mystery meat. *Tomorrow I'm brown bagging it.*

"You didn't have to pick up trash," Spike said. "I sweated my balls off all summer."

I started to say, "You never had any to begin with," and Spike looked at me like he was expecting me to say it. Truth was, though, he and the other guys *did* have balls. They'd gamely volunteered to play their first (and last) underground gig over the MemeCast on the eve of July First, the day the mandatory chips went into effect.

I gave Spike's hand a squeeze instead. The boy actually blushed.

"After the rally today, I'm officially off duty," I told him, leaning toward him ever so slightly. I couldn't resist teasing a bit—but only a bit. Spike was always there for me. Even if he didn't remember.

"Us, too," Richie spoke up for the first time. "Band practice?"

Steven nodded his head vigorously. Spike sighed, and I had to laugh. I let go of his hand and tried a fry.

"Want to join us?" I asked Micah.

"I told Winter I'd drop by her grandfather's." Micah wiped his plate longingly with his last fry. I pushed my pudding toward him.

"Is she back living with him?" I hoped it was true just so I could see her more. Tamarind Bay, where her parents lived now, was a long, long walk (or an increasingly expensive bus ride) from my part of town.

"No," Micah explained. "But everything is cool between all the Nomuras again. And you know Winter; she's always got a project going." With a glance at the security cameras, he leaned in and whispered, "You guys should see the latest one. Come with me after school."

"Maybe Mr. Yamada will let us practice there," I said. Winter's grandfather had a huge old converted warehouse space with a funky outdoor area. And it was in a part of town where none of the neighbors would be bothered by a band that needed a lot of practice. "It'll be cooler than Spike's garage." *And we can talk about what really happened at the rave—and after. How much did the boys remember? Did Winter and Aiden tell Micah and Nora what we'd been planning that night? Did it work?*

I had the nagging feeling I was forgetting something important.

Lights flickered off and the meager AC stopped blowing. A siren blared and a pale emergency light snapped on over the back door, the one that led to the stoner area. Spike's hand reached for mine under the table—but I wasn't thinking about him.

10.0

THERE MUST BE SOME WAY OUT OF HERE

VELVET

In the darkness, lit only by the flashing emergency light, all I could see was the kid in the lime green T-shirt. That didn't make sense. I'd seen him in broad daylight. But he'd begun to haunt my dreams—along with those damned paper coffins. I dug my nails into Spike's hand without really meaning to. He led us outside to the stoner area.

"What's wrong, babe?" he asked quietly as we settled under the tree by the fence.

I shook my head. "I'll tell you later" was all I could manage. Though it was hotter, I felt instantly better outside and away from the flashing light. Stephen tuned in to a 'cast on his mobile. I laid my head against Spike's shoulder and almost fell asleep. But I could still hear the newsranter blathering on about how the Coalition was to blame for all the shortages.

The blackout lasted only twenty minutes—just long enough for the guys to finish their lunches outside. I felt like a zombie the rest of the day. The only thing that kept me going was the thought of seeing Winter after the Mignon rally. I couldn't get away with skipping it, but the guys said they'd wait for me.

So there I sat in the bleachers with the other "volunteers" when Mignon rolled in. After a bunch of yada yada from Buffy McCheerleader and our esteemed principal, Mignon started talking. The usual stuff. Freedom. Security. Patriotism. I kind of zoned out at that point. Until he started talking about service overseas and our troops keeping us safe at home.

I sincerely hope he doesn't turn this into a recruiting session.

One Kowalcyk in the military was one too many. Dad joined the army after high school and after the Golden Gate thing. He's done tours in Venezuela and all over the Middle East. I can't even keep them straight. *Just follow the trail of oil*, Dad always said. *They ain't making any more of it.*

Mignon called out a name. Rachel Gearhardt. Everyone looked around, and Rachel tentatively stood up. She was a senior with beautiful auburn hair down to her butt. Practically. She was on the basketball team and a

Merit scholar on top of that. A tall woman in desert camo walked into the gym and took off her cover (her cap, for you non-military brats). Wisps of red hair escaped from the neat ponytail tucked into her collar.

"Mom!" screamed the normally reserved Rachel as she leaped down the bleachers.

Hugging and crying ensued, while Mignon yammered over the reunion. Though I was happy for Rachel and her mom, who turned out to be a bird colonel, it felt like a cheap stunt. Probably half the school had a parental in the military, and most of us were trying not to think "why not my mom or dad?"

Our sacrifices keep them safe.

For half a second, the image of my dad's name on a paper coffin flashed through my brain. TRAVIS K. I dreamt this last night. My foot was stuck in the cardboard, and this time his name was on it instead of mine.

My hands started shaking, and the cavernous gym seemed like it was closing in on me. I slipped from my seat quietly and snuck out of the gym while the mayor did a photo opp with the Gearhardts. I ran outside, zipping my hoodie back up as my boot heels clacked against the pavement.

I slumped down in the first shady spot in front of the school, a giant oak planted a hundred years ago.

Maybe I need to go to TFC. I expected the nightmares, but not this crap. Dad has nightmares. Last time he was home, I heard him yelling in his sleep. Probably the whole neighborhood heard him. When Mom pressed him, he said he'd go to counseling at the VA, but they wanted him to go to TFC. Free of charge for vets. He said he'd never go.

I pulled out my notebook and started writing. Mostly images from my dreams. Maybe I could trap them in my notebook or in a song and they'd leave me alone at night. I wrote that thought down, too.

The next thing I knew, Spike and the guys were standing in front of me. "You okay?" Micah asked as he passed me a bottle of cold water.

"I just couldn't take the bullshit anymore," I said after I gulped it down greedily. "Let's get the hell out of here."

11.0

ONCE MORE INTO THE GARDEN

VELVET

The heat rose in rivulets off the pavement as we walked, and that ungodly warmth permeated up through my sneakers, crawled in prickles over my tights, and settled right under my sweatshirt. I felt like the cheap plastic letters of VOTE MIGNON were burning into my chest like a brand.

Walking in a black hoodie in late afternoon across the urban heat sink of September is never a good idea. *Book of Velvet.*

But I wasn't taking it off. I wasn't about to flash my hideous Mignon T-shirt.

Spike took my sweaty palm in his hand. Richie and Little Steven walked in front of us talking about music and gigs. Micah trailed behind, lost in his own little world.

". . . Chuck Martin is turning eighteen soon," Richie, the business tycoon of the band, said. The Wannabes played everything from bar mitzvahs to graduation parties. "He wants us to play—"

"Wasn't he one of guys who beat up Micah last year?" I interrupted. Martin and a few other football jocks had jumped Micah after a game last fall.

Spike nodded.

"But a gig's a gig," Richie countered. "He'll understand."

Steven shrugged. "We could play those Lo-Fi covers we worked on."

I glanced back at Micah, but he didn't seem to be listening.

"Did you know that 'Curb' wasn't their first song?" Spike tossed in. I could see what was coming. A little rock trivia smackdown. I slipped my hand from Spike's. He launched into quizzing the other guys about the Lo-Fi Strangers' first tour, the name of the girl mentioned in "Mayhem Remembers," and other such arcane, useless trivia.

I fell back in step with Micah.

"So that was a very small towel you had on the other day," I said after a few steps.

"And that's a very yellow shirt you're trying to hide."

We both laughed.

"So what happened to you and Nora, you know, after?" When I'd gotten escorted out of the rave, Micah and Nora were still hidden under the stage.

"You remember that?" He shifted the weight of his ever-present messenger bag.

"Remember what?" I smiled oh so innocently.

"But those guys—" Micah motioned to Spike and the boys.

I shrugged. I knew what he meant, though. The guys had holes in their memories about that night. I'd figured that out from talking to Spike. "If you want to hang on to precious memories these days, lie your butt off. *Book of Velvet*. Chapter 73, Verse 1."

It took him a second to process it. We all knew the TFC spiel. The memory-erasing drug required you to activate the memories by telling your story; then the drug blocked the memory re-sticking process. But if you didn't tell the truth or omitted key parts—

"Dude," Micah said with a low, appreciative whistle. "How did you know it would work?"

"I didn't." Maybe I'm immune to the blab juice or they didn't bother giving me any. That whole misunderestimation thing. Or maybe I gave them an earful of shit they didn't want to hear. Maybe I blabbed about an old boyfriend I wanted to forget. Bottom line: I remembered everything that mattered. The plan. The band. My friends.

I started to turn on Eighth but Micah pointed up ahead. "Back door."

All I saw was a chain-link fence covered with Nomura Electronics signs. It had to be Mr. Yamada's yard.

Micah slid the sign aside and placed his thumb on a lockpad. The chain-link fence slid to the right, revealing the space under the bleachers in Mr. Yamada's Sasuke course.

"I usually knock on the front door," I said flatly, impressed—and, I had to admit, a tad jealous at his access to Winter's house. Well, I guess it was just her grandfather's home now.

"Mr. Yamada lets me skate or crash here sometimes."

Winter had, of course, told me that. I felt bad for bringing it up.

The other guys made guffawing sounds as we emerged from under the bleachers onto the Sasuke course. It's this crazy cool obstacle course Mr. Yamada had built years ago based on some Japanese game show. The course was a giant playground of steel, Plexiglas, wood, and rope. Dad said it sounded like a Confidence Course, an obstacle course you had to pass in basic training. But the obstacles were a little crazier than just climbing a wall or swinging over a ditch. Mr. Yamada had this log thing you held on to as you zip-lined across a shallow pond to a cargo net.

Do not try this in a skirt. *Book of Velvet*. Chapter 47, Verse 12.

I am full of wisdom (or something) today.

The log ride and the Warped Wall were still intact, but—

"Something's different," I blurted out. There were several somethings actually. There was an odd sculpture atop the Spider Climb, this Plexiglas tower you were supposed to shinny. Its sides were now covered in solar panels. And plants grew out of the bleachers, blooms spilling over the seats like a cascade. Greens and herbs and a few flowers were now the only spectators of Mr. Yamada's game show. The air was thick with new earth, rosemary, lavender, and a hint of garlic.

"One of Mr. Yamada's new projects. He figures the space is better used for food and power. I did convince him to keep the Warped Wall, though." Micah pointed to the obstacle that most resembled a skateboard ramp. Typical.

"Hey, the shit is going to hit the fan. You gotta be ready," Steven spoke up with more animation than I'd seen from him all day.

"Only those with money can afford to prepare for when there isn't going to be any. *Book of Velvet*," I said.

The other guys laughed, but Little Steven looked positively grim.

For some of us, shit had hit the fan long ago. Mom's been doing the community gardening and bartering thing for ages. Dad's army pay doesn't go far, and we live in a crap neighborhood where there isn't even a grocery store anymore. *Maybe Winter could help us out with a solar panel or two*.

I pushed open the smooth bamboo gate at the other end of the Sasuke course and held it open for the guys. They didn't guffaw this time. Stunned silence was the only thing that came out of their gaping pie holes. Except for Micah's, of course. He'd seen the garden a million times. Probably more than I had, come to think of it.

Winter's garden hadn't changed much since June. The smooth bamboo walks still criss-crossed through a sea of white sand. Winter's sculptures still bobbed, turned, reached, crawled, and flapped in the sun. A pagoda still sat in the center.

And in it, Winter and Lina (aka Lanky Girl from the Rocket Garden crew) were intently tinkering with something on the table. Eerie music played from the Sail Cloth sculpture as sunlight moved across the garden. Winter called it her solar chimes. Annoying, grating pseudo elevator music, I called it. The sculpture really was a big radio receiver, she'd explained once upon a time. She had her own low-power transmitter in the shop—hidden in a vintage Scooby Doo lunchbox, of all things. Her Scooby Doo rig was the same kind as the one Rebecca Starr used to transmit the MemeCast, only she'd hidden hers in a bakery truck with a big black dog on the side.

Micah cleared his throat and stepped aside to reveal me.

Ta-freaking-da.

Winter and Lina stared at me for a moment. Lina had also been at the rave, but I'd seen her get out. She'd been working the door. She hit the alarm the second she'd seen (or heard) black vans roll up outside, and got away. I think Big Steven did, too. I wondered if our Steven has seen his big brother since then. (Yes, both brothers were Stevens, Big and Little. Contrary to popular opinion, their dad—also named Steven—was not some narcissistic tool who insisted on naming all his kids after himself. Little Steven had been adopted at three or four, and nobody, especially him, liked his middle name, Marion.)

Winter was peering at me now with her X-ray eyes, no doubt trying to figure out how empty my head was. I let her sweat for a few more seconds.

"Well, did it work?" I hooked my thumb at the Sail Cloth sculpture. "Are your parents okay? Did we cleanse the hearts and minds of the greater downtown area? Or did we get busted for nothing?"

Spike and the boys looked at me with blank, what-gives expressions plastered across their faces.

"Babe, what are you talking about?" Spike asked, his hand touching the small of my back.

Winter leaped to her feet and actually hugged me. She's not usually Miss Bodily Contact. At all. Lina glowered at me. And I understood instantly. I only hoped Winter felt the same way about her.

Winter started explaining everything at a hundred miles an hour.

And that nagging feeling returned.

I had forgotten something.

SKYNET, MINUS ALL THE TERMINATORS, MAYBE.

AIDEN

Jao pulled up outside Mr. Yamada's house just as the call went through. Mom and I finally connected.

"I'll be home as soon as I can, *mäuschen*," my mother said sleepily. It was nearly eleven in Zurich. "I can't say much, but we still have the Riyad crisis to deal with. How's school? How's your internship project?"

"Boring, and okay." She expected the former, and I knew I couldn't say more about the latter. It had taken me a few days of cold calling on a modded mobile, one I'd hacked to show it was coming from a TFC exchange, to finally find a junior-level database admin at city hall who gave me want I wanted: the name and address of the ID chip database. People will tell their own tech support anything.

The hack might not hold, but it was a start. We'd beta test it on a few willing guinea pigs first.

The universe muttered, and I told Mom to go back to sleep. At least I'd heard from one of the two women I worried about.

"Jao, you can go home," I said. He just grunted and turned up his favorite sportscast.

The universe warned me again as soon as I opened Mr. Yamada's front door.

Winter was talking so fast it almost sounded like the wings of a hummingbird. Almost.

And she was there.

And this guy had his hand on her butt.

Velvet, standing there in a very Velvet outfit, looked at me.

And that little voice I call the universe started muttering again.

All the while, Winter was still explaining something—the rave aftermath, I think—in her own rapid-fire way.

Slowly, it dawned on me. I looked at Micah, and he gave me a confirming nod. Velvet was still Velvet.

The thought made me stupidly happy. Golden. Glossy even.

And I didn't even mind that the guy leaned in and whispered something in her ear, something that made her laugh.

I tried to suppress an idiotic grin. Epic fail.

And she grinned back.

And that, thankfully, shut Winter up. She glared at me and Velvet for interrupting her flow.

Then, as if on cue, Winter's creepy chimes all of a sudden intoned, "You've got mail."

I can't believe she went there. Sometimes I forget Winter does have a sense of humor. "That's way too old school," I told her. But appropriate. It's the sound one of the first popular e-mail programs made whenever you got a message. Back in the day when you had to use the telephone lines to access the Internet. Back in the day when we had hard lines.

Winter darted into the workshop without replying. And I was right behind her, with Micah and Lina pulling up the rear. Winter turned on the tiny screen attached to an ancient tan computer that was Node Zero, the gateway server for the fledgling MemeNet. Her fingers clattered over the old keyboard.

"It's from Nora." Winter grinned. That meant Nora's node was online and connected to ours via a string of other nodes.

I checked the stats on my jailbroken mobile. I'd set certain far-flung nodes to ping us when they came online. Hers was date-stamped eighteen hours ago. We were just getting the message now because the chain of nodes between here and Los Palamos hadn't been complete (or they hadn't all been on) until now. I'd actually been out placing a few new ones on my way over from Tamarind

Bay. I showed Winter the network map of active nodes. It was a glittering web of gorgeosity extending almost to the city limits and beyond in some places.

"That's where Big Steven was going," Lina said, peering over my shoulder. She pointed to a pulsing point just outside the city limits. Big Steven and some new recruits were working their way from Hamilton to DC.

Micah pointed to a few pinpricks of light along the river. "I'll take some more boxes down there this week," he said. "How many do we have?"

On the map, there was just a park. We needed some in that general area to connect the dots between other areas. But it seemed a waste to put any more precious hotspots down there. I shook my head. "You should go to one of these neighborhoods—where there are people." I let a little sarcasm seep into my voice.

"There are *plenty* of people in Thomas Park," Micah replied patiently, as if I were the idiot. Winter and Lina both confirmed that with a look. "Hundreds," Micah continued. "They live there. Work there. Trade there." Micah then proceeded to enlighten me. It seems that Thomas Park was where those who fell (or jumped) off the security grid went. And a whole underground economy was growing there. "Mr. Kim said he'll hook the other vendors up with hotspots. He can also pass out some to residents."

Putting hotspots in the traders' stalls made sense, but I was still filled with dubiosity about giving routers to the homeless. I hesitated, not sure how to put it delicately. Finally, I asked, "What does that buy us?" Don't think I succeeded with the delicate part.

"We need to spread those dots over a wide area, right?" Micah motioned to a still dark portion of the map. "Homeless people get around—and into areas that most people don't go," Micah said.

I had a feeling he was talking from experience. Winter had told me that Micah and his mother lived out of a car for a while before they moved into a homeless village at Black Dog Salvage. Which got trashed by the city.

"And they can pass them to dozens of others," he added.

Okay, now I had to admit his idea wasn't as bogus as I'd thought. I could see the pinpricks of light moving across the city. The map reminded me of the one I'd seen in that TFC in Bern. Its red dots showed the spread of new TFCs sprouting across the face of Europe. Like a rash. Or a plague.

The universe muttered something incomprehensible.

"You take as many routers down there as you can—as soon as you can," I told Micah. A thought popped into my head. I turned to Lina. "Could you make wearable hotspots?" Lina was all about melding electronics and textiles.

"Genius," Lina practically squealed.

"Dude," Micah exclaimed. "That would be so much easier for the gridless—"

Someone cleared her throat behind us. I'd almost forgotten it wasn't just the four of us, like it had been for the last two months.

Velvet stood there, arms crossed, a bemused look on her face. The other guys were arrayed behind her. "Care to let us techno-peons in on the excitement?"

I grinned like an idiot again, but she only raised an eyebrow at me. I should've hugged her, but now that guy had his arm protectively around her waist.

Deep breath. Don't think about that now. Focus. Make intelligent words come out of your mouth. "We've been building our own internet," I finally said.

Dead silence. Which was only broken by someone's stomach growling loudly. Mine answered.

Winter and Velvet played hostess while Lina and I ran a connection test. The speed wasn't consistent. But another node came online while we watched the results spew across the screen. One of the other guys, possibly Big Steven's brother, hovered behind us. I think he wanted to ask us something, but Velvet kicked the door from the workshop open and carried in a tray of coffee mugs.

"Hey, watch it. Sasuke-san will not be happy if you bruise his house, V," Winter snapped at her. She was carrying a plate of cookies.

"Okay, spill," Velvet said once we'd all gotten a few sips of coffee—and in the guys' cases, a half-dozen cookies in our mouths. She'd changed into a Lego T-shirt,

Winter's obviously, and it was a little tight in places where my cousin was definitely flatter.

"Hello?" Velvet said.

"Yeah," I said to cover my distraction. "You know how the MemeCast used old radio waves no one was using anymore? Well, we're building on that. We're using other frequencies—ones that used to be used for wireless networking—and setting up nodes to bounce signals off of." I rambled on about how these nodes—routers and gateways—only had a certain range, so we had to string a bunch together to get a message from one side of town to the other.

"It's how dissidents used to talk to each other in countries where the government shut off Internet access," Lina jumped in, trying to pull my rambling back on course.

Didn't work. My mouth kept explaining how shadow networks had started back in the day, before the Internet went entirely corporate.

"I get it; the MemeNet bypasses the security grid," Velvet cut me off. "But why did it take so long for a message to get from Los Palamos to here? That doesn't seem too practical."

"Since we're still building our network, we didn't have the nodes online between here and there until just now." I showed Velvet the map, too. There was a big hole in the coverage south of town. "So if a message is sent from here to there, the message has to wait there." I pointed to the last node in the line.

"Kind of like the Pony Express waiting for fresh horses, huh?" Velvet asked, her fingers touching the map—and mine. "Or maybe nerve cells growing."

"Exactly." The lag time would disappear as the MemeNet covered the city, and the next, and the next. More nodes meant more routes a message could take.

"It's like our own Skynet," Velvet's guy friend—Spike, I now remembered—interjected. "Minus the Terminators, of course."

We can only hope, the universe muttered in the back of my head.

A LIFE COUNTED IN WEEKENDS

NORA

It was only mid-September, and I was already living for the weekend, which was so not me. I used to be the girl who lived for planning photo spreads in yearbooks, gossiping in the hall with my glossy-headed girls, sitting at the right lunch table, and going to committee meetings. Now I cruised through the halls of Los Palamos High on autopilot, as if I were just visiting. Oh, I acted like the old Nora. I went to class, mouthed all the right words to the right people, did my homework, and even cheered at the pep rally. Go Palominos! But I was just sleepwalking through the day.

But Friday afternoons, when the car left the LP gates, I woke up. Those evenings, Mom and I would cook dinner and watch a movie. Saturdays, Micah and I would hang out, either at Mr. Yamada's or at some mall and coffee shop within a bus ride of downtown. We used our dates as cover to spread little white boxes around the greater Hamilton area.

Too bad it was a Tuesday night.

The click of my new low-slung heels against the marble echoed in the apartment. The usual note from Dad said he'd be home really late and to eat without him. Even when he was home, I hardly saw him. He was usually holed up in his office working or on some overseas call that I was not supposed to disturb.

Opening the fridge, I stared at the meticulously clean and organized contents. Two rows of diet sodas. One carton of skim milk. An OJ. Nine strawberry yogurts. Two take-out containers with dates penciled across the top. (The maid did that and would toss them after three days.) And a vegetable crisper full of Lowenberger beer. It was the only dietary evidence that someone else besides me lived here. I grabbed a can of soda and pulled a Lean & Fit out of the freezer door. Chicken portabella. The picture made it look way better than I knew it was going to taste. Still.

The AC hummed in the quiet of the apartment. Dad absolutely, positively said I could not have a cat.

I flicked on a music 'cast to fill up the silence. Mom called to check in and see how I did on my *Grapes of Wrath* paper.

I got an A. Also so not me.

"Why are you home so late?" she asked as I stuck the package tray in the microwave.

"Dad signed me up for a prep class for the SATs and stuff." The woman coached you on what classes to take, which extracurriculars to do, what AP classes to take, how to write killer college essays, and generally how to get into your dream college. The hour was excruciatingly dreary.

Mom was silent for a moment. "I guess that's a good thing; it'll help you get in wherever you want to go. Hope you're having something other than takeout, though."

I read her the ingredients from the package of chicken portabella.

"Oh, honey, next weekend we'll cook some extra meals for you to take home." She was washing something in the sink of her tiny kitchen.

Oddly, I looked forward to that. Friday nights we usually made lasagna or real chicken together. I removed my "dinner" from the microwave and poked a rubbery, beige piece of something with a fork. I wasn't sure if it was chicken or mushroom, even after I tasted it.

"Those look good," I said, gazing longingly at the bright red and yellow peppers she was now chopping for a stir-fry.

"Some of my clients pay in currency other than cash," she said with a wink.

We chit-chatted a little more about homework and her cases—the same type of thing we talked about while cooking dinner on Friday evenings. It was nice. We'd never really done much of this before she'd left Dad. We used to bond over shopping; now it was food. No, it was more than that. Or less. I don't know.

After we hung up, I put a repeat of *Judge Tootie* on the screen and cracked open my algebra book. I did my homework while I polished off a strawberry yogurt and another Diet Coke. I texted Micah. He was re-reading his favorite graphic novel of all time, *Maus*. It was the story of the artist guy's father surviving a Nazi concentration camp. Dreary reading, if you ask me.

Jews are mice; the Nazi's cats, Micah texted, before he signed off.

I wasn't sure why this book fascinated him, but there was something really familiar about the conversation, like we'd had it before, and it made me think of *Memento*.

I cleaned up the kitchen, locked my bedroom door, and pulled out my secret stash of *Memento*s from between the mattress and box spring. (Mom had saved them for me.)

The black-and-white pages still had that new smell to them. I spread them out on the bed and read them as if I'd never seen them before.

The first issued showed me going to TFC for the first time and hearing the memory Mom wanted to erase: Dad slamming her face into a doorframe. I spit the pill out so I could remember.

Another issue showed Micah getting hit by a black van

as it sped away from the bookstore bombing. In another, the black van guys were planting a bomb on a car that had a kid in it. Micah raps on the window and gets the kid out in the nick of time. The van heads back to Soft Target, my dad's old firm, as the car blows up.

I didn't remember working on these with Micah, exactly. I do recall a feeling, though—one I still get when I look at the sheets of paper. It's this warm feeling in my chest. Like an overwhelming sense of having really done something—something good. It's almost as if what's on the paper is real, and my here-and-now is the dream. Except on the weekends. And maybe that's not enough.

I texted Micah—over our Nomura Freedoms, of course—*We need to do Memento again.*

He didn't reply.

14.0

THE DANGER OF MAGICAL THINKING

NORA

Saturday was a dreary, rainy, late September day. Outside, that is. Mom was with a client downstairs, and Micah and I were watching some military love story thing on the big screen—well, what passed for a big screen at Mom's place. We had popcorn and sodas. And he had his arm around me as we sat on the lumpy, brown, secondhand sofa.

On screen, the officer barked out orders to his soldiers before they attacked an insurgent village. The two secret lovers, serving in the same unit, stole a meaningful glance at each other before they strapped on their M16's. The scene flashed to the night before, when Henry and Celine stole more than a glance. One of them probably wasn't coming back from this action. An ad for the army scrolled across the bottom of the screen.

"Isn't it funny how Winter and Aiden have become like behind-the-scenes generals or something?" Micah asked as he reached for the popcorn.

"Hilarious," I replied, changing the movie to a music 'cast. Typical for a guy to focus on that part of the scene. He was right. Aiden and Winter had us planting hotspots and handing out Nomura Freedoms all over town for the past few weekends. The rain had finally given us a break just to hang out.

"What?"

I sighed. The boy was clueless.

"Didn't you have some sketches you wanted to show me?" I muted the ad for Vigilance car service.

Micah grabbed his sketch pad out of his bag. He flipped it open to a scene outside TFC No. 23. People were carrying tiny coffins with names on them. Then black vans rolled up, and guys in gas masks blasted the protestors with tear gas. Micah explained what he'd seen. He stabbed his finger at the last frame where the cop was rolling up her window and he was running away, his eyes burning. "And they just sat there," he choked out the words.

This seemed so familiar, the two of us talking and looking at sketches. I reached out and touched his hand. And before I knew it, I was kissing him. He tasted salty and sweet. He ran his hand through my hair and touched my neck lightly. I felt a very glossy shiver run through me. I could've kissed him all evening, but the thought of my mom coming back upstairs popped into my mind. As did something else. Something I'd been thinking about all week. I pulled my lips gently away from his. I suppressed a giggle because his glasses had fogged up.

"This would make a great issue of *Memento*," I said, pointing to the sketches. He'd never answered my text about it, though we'd chatted about everything else over the last three days. "Aiden says the MemeNet is ready. He's already put the old comics up." I pulled out the hard copies from my bag.

Micah turned away from me to wipe off his glasses. "I don't know, Nora," he said after polishing his lens to a high gloss. "We did get caught last time."

"We're way less likely to get caught on the MemeNet," I said, but I wasn't sure if I believed it.

Micah shrugged and unmuted the music. I got it—what he didn't want to say. We were both caught last time, but *he* went to juvie. *He* served community service. *His* home got broken up. My home may have broken up, too, in a whole other way. But I got a trip to the beach, a charm bracelet, and a penthouse apartment.

"It's okay," I said. I leaned over and kissed him again. We'd hear Mom when she unlocked the door, I told myself. He didn't kiss me back at first, but finally he did. Micah took his glasses off this time.

The Action News 'cast broke into our music. Micah reached for the remote, but I stopped him. It was Rebecca Starr and her new show, sadly called the MemeCast.

"A local woman is suing the TFC corporation for the

records of her visits so she can use them in a custody hearing. . . ."

I turned up the sound.

Micah groaned and put his glasses back on.

"It's about my mom," I told him.

Rebecca Starr talked up the human-interest side. A young woman with a child, trying to keep her family together, sacrificed her safety and dignity for the sake of her daughter. Now that she's able to stand on her own—

I clicked it off. I knew deep down she'd done it for me, but I'd never heard her say it. It was ten times worse hearing it from a stranger.

"What was that about?" Micah put his arm around me again. It made me feel protected. Somewhat.

I told him. Mom had gone ahead with my crazy idea. TFC had turned down her request for her session records, and now she was suing for them in order to use them in the custody suit.

"Does she actually think they'd give her the real files?" Micah asked incredulously. He got it.

"Exactly!" Mom must know they won't. She says she wants to force the issue, remind people of the kind of memories they might be giving up. Deep down, though, I think she's hoping it'll magically work and justice will prevail. Or that Dad will give up the custody fight.

"What if we did a *Memento* on Mom's suit?" I asked hesitantly. That might help others not make the same mistake. I pulled out a pad of paper where I'd already started writing the script.

Micah didn't answer or even look at what I'd written. He murmured that he had to get home. Then he packed his stuff and took off.

I shouldn't have pushed it, I guess. But I hoped he got soaked on the way home.

REALITY BYTES

MICAH

I dropped my skateboard to the curb and pushed off. The rain quickly soaked me but I didn't care. I took the long way home through the back alleys.

Even before Nora mentioned it, I had been thinking about drawing more *Memento*s—when the MemeNet was fully online. But that happened so fast. It's only been a few weeks. And Aiden has already moved the Meme-Cast to the shadow network. Velvet and the boys already played some of their songs over it. But I keep putting off *Memento*. Maybe I never expected the thing to actually grow like it has.

Then last weekend, Aiden and Winter got a message from some dude they knew who was doing the same thing in another city up the coast. And he had other people doing the same thing in other cities. Pings and messages came rolling in from Portland, Maine; New York City; and Jacksonville, Florida.

All of a sudden this underground network was so freaking real, and it was a whole lot more serious than putting a hand-printed comic in the school bathroom.

And I had more to lose this time around, too. A place to live, a girl who was maybe a little more than a friend.

And that scared the crap out of me.

I am such a chickenshit douche.

Nora deserved better, especially considering her whole dad thing.

I stopped outside my building and sent Nora a message. *Sorry. Let me think about it.*

My Freedom vibrated. I expected a message from Nora saying it was okay or something sweet and understanding like she always said. But the message said "Jonas W. lives." That was it. The sender was anonymous.

I did a 180 and banked my board toward Mr. Yamada's, hoping to catch Winter.

Aiden was there recording his latest show.

"Sorry, man," Aiden said when I showed the message to him. "We designed the MemeNet for real anonymity. I can tell the general path the message took—but it could've come from outside anywhere."

This lit a fire under my butt. I had to find out what happened to my dad and whether he was still alive.

And the logical place to start was with my mom.

16.0

THE GAS-LIGHTING OF HOMELAND HIGH

MICAH

Our place was quiet and hot. Just the way Mr. Mao liked it. The cat was stretched out in one of the lawn chairs we were using for living room furniture.

Mom was working another double shift. That meant she wouldn't be home until noon—tomorrow. She used to pull doubles all the time when we didn't have a place. She was saving up for first and last month's rent plus the hefty security deposits some places required if you had a shit security score. Something always came up, though. A medical bill. Clothes for school. Food. And most places wouldn't rent to you at all unless you had a score over 600 anyway. Mom never said how bad ours was.

Now she pulled doubles to pay for this place.

I nudged the AC down a few more degrees and surveyed the contents of the fridge. White bread. Green peppers. Three juice boxes. In the cabinet, I spied two cans of chicken noodle soup and one can of Wheelios.

We were better off in Black Dog Village. I was, anyway. Someone was always around. I could contribute by building things, or helping Mr. Shaw salvage old houses, or carting firewood for Mrs. B's bake ovens. I wish I knew where Mrs. Brooks was. She'd know what to do about this dad thing—or she'd bake me a muffin and tell me *not* to do whatever stupid thing I was thinking of doing.

So I did something stupid. I crawled into bed with Mr. Mao, a bowl of wagon-wheel-shaped spaghetti, and a juice box. (Not the stupid part.) I pulled out my mobile—my real, on-the-security-grid one—and searched for information on Jonas Wallenberg. I'd done this years ago and gotten nada. It was like he hadn't existed. This time, though, I got a hit. A short entry:

Jonas M. Wallenberg. Terrorist. Further information classified.

I blinked at the screen. *No.* That couldn't be true. It's a lie. But a hot, stinking feeling of shame washed over me.

A little voice somewhere in my head whispered, *You knew it all along. That's why your security score is so low.* Another voice said, *You don't have to be like him.*

It did make a certain sick sense. Mom had lost her job

at a big regional hospital, then we'd lost the house, then the shabby apartment. Nothing could tank your security score faster than being married to a terrorist. Or being the son of one.

The sound of the old-fashioned alarm clock by my bed ticked loudly, too loudly in the deathly quiet of the apartment.

I shoved my pasta toward Mr. Mao and dug my skateboard out from under the bed. I needed to do something, and I couldn't sit still to draw. Curfew be damned.

I skated down the back alleys of the city, careful to avoid people (and cameras). It was after curfew now, but I'd spent a lot of my homeless days (nights, actually) skating under the radar while Mom worked. We'd even lived out of a car for a while—and that's no place to spend a hot, sticky evening in this city. A ghost of a memory flitted across my mind. I was seeing black van guys tagging a car. Then I was pounding on the window to roust out some young kid—right before the car blew up. I couldn't tell if I remembered it or if I was remembering the drawing I'd done in *Memento*.

I soon found myself at Mr. Yamada's back gate.

No one seemed to be home. Winter and Aiden were probably at their swank homes in Tamarind Bay with their families. Maybe Mr. Y. was there, too. Or he was working late. Or he was with friends. What did old people do? I wondered. Cool old guys, that is.

So I skated the Warped Wall a few times. I dropped

off the lower platform and pushed off hard. I tucked in, trying to get up the speed to ride the wave of wall upward to the top platform. I'd seen Mr. Yamada do it just by running hundreds of times. He could stretch himself out at the last second and grab the top with his fingertips and pull himself up in one, fluid motion. I missed the top and slid back down to the bottom on my behind. I tried a few more times with the same results before I decided just to lie there at the bottom of the curl, board under my head, watching the stars.

I had the dream again. I was in a big crowd—actually, just above it. The scene was always a little out of focus. It was one of those warm, sticky evenings. I could smell cut grass and damp earth. Music was playing, and people swayed all around us. I was sitting on my father's shoulders, watching. Then there was shouting, and Dad was putting me up high somewhere or maybe handing me to someone up on the stage. The crowd swallowed him up, and he was gone.

Something splatted onto my forehead.

"Micah?"

My eyes flickered open as a few more droplets of water dripped onto my face. Again. Mr. Yamada was dressed in jeans, a black SASUKE INK T-shirt, and his usual fedora—and he was holding a hose.

"I'm up!" I rolled to my feet before he could fully water me.

After helping him water the plants and eating half his

scrambled eggs, I broke down and told Mr. Yamada what I'd found out.

"I heard your father speak once," he said, taking an agonizing pause to sip his tea. "Must have been fifteen years ago, right before the riots."

"You knew him?"

"No, I was just one of hundreds there listening to him. Your dad was organizing protests against TFC. That was back when the clinics first opened."

"Why didn't you ever tell me?" Had I been dreaming about one of those protests?

Mr. Yamada shrugged. "I'm not sure."

"Who else knew my dad?"

He shrugged again. "My memory is a little fuzzy, Micah. I'm sorry."

Of course, Mr. Yamada had gone to Detention, too.

"I should get to the shop—and you need to get to school." He tossed me an apple. "Maybe I should plant a tree by the Curtain Cling."

I got to school late, even on my skateboard, and everyone gave me the stinkeye when I slipped into homeroom. I grabbed a seat in the back, and Jessica Wilson actually moved. I smelled my pits. Yes, I could've used some Guy Code this morning.

Homeland Teen News jabbered on about how running for school office looks good on college applications. I tried hard to listen because half the class was cutting looks at me. I stared straight ahead at the screen. The army advertised for a few more good men (and women) with the added incentive of bonus pay. And the world news segment said something about the Coalition bombing in Norway (or was it the North Sea?) being linked to someplace in Africa. Or did she say Arabia? I was having trouble concentrating with everyone eyeballing me.

Terrorism was still on the rise, the news gal said. Again. Funny how it always seemed to happen around elections.

I could feel every single eye in the classroom on me.

Your father was a terrorist, a little voice whispered in my head.

The bell rang and I shot out of there.

All day people were glaring and whispering around me. Or moving away from me. I got more than the usual bumpage in the hallway from the jocks—including Chuck Martin and the other football players. Spike wouldn't even look in my direction in Spanish. And my teachers called on me repeatedly in every class, and in the same tone, pronounced "Mr. Wallenberg" as if I were some strange new insect or had the plague. Normally, I manage to fly pretty low under the radar at school.

And then came lunch. The usual din of the cafeteria fell to a hush as I walked in. The lunch lady sullenly told me she was out of pizza when there was clearly half a pie in front of her. I grabbed a random sandwich and juice box from the ready-made counter and practically bolted toward my table.

What the heck was going on?

My crew was very intent on the food on their plates. I sat down and discovered I had an egg salad sandwich and a fruit punch. I hated them both—almost as much as I hated this day.

My friends said nothing. And they had pizza, every one of them.

"What? Am I covered in turd today or something?" I slammed down my sandwich in disgust.

Your father betrayed his country.

Velvet looked up at me and blurted out, "No, but your dad was a terrorist."

I stared at my friends.

The voice in my head was telling me something I knew wasn't true.

Spike pushed his plate away and finally looked at me. "Yeah, dude, how come you never mentioned it?"

"I only just found out," I stammered. "And it can't be true." I explained what had happened and what Mr. Yamada said. "So how did you know? Did you suddenly just remember?"

Velvet and the boys nodded. Everybody at Homeland High suddenly just remembered.

We all came to same conclusion. It was the ID chips. I'd triggered something with my search last night, and now TFC was feeding me and everyone at Homeland High No. 17 the same crap.

"'All that you remember may not be the truth,'"

Velvet quoted. She explained for those of us with Swiss cheese memories that it was something Meme Girl had said when she first warned everyone about the ID chips.

I texted Nora, but she didn't remember anything about my dad.

When I got home, Mom was waiting for me. She was still in her scrubs and looked like she hadn't slept yet. She slipped a plate of bacon and eggs in front of me and headed toward her room. She paused at the door. "Your father was not a terrorist—no matter what anyone or anything tells you."

She wouldn't, or maybe couldn't, say anymore. She went to bed.

In the morning, Mom was looking for a new job. Everyone at Sunny Oaks Retirement Home suddenly remembered Jonas Wallenberg, too.

They shouldn't have done that. I kicked off my board hard toward school, or wherever. I repeated the things I knew in my gut to be true.

One. My dad was not a terrorist.

Two. We suddenly had a whole lot less to lose.

I texted Nora one word: *Memento*.

MemeCast 2.5—
MEET THE MEMES

Okay, citizens. Neo here. Trinity303 has been plaguing me with questions. Great ones like this: Why the Meme-Cast? Or the MemeNet? Aren't memes those pics of cats or monkeys with dumb quotes that we annoy the heck out of each other with 'cause we have nothing better to do?

Yes and no, Trin. First of all, I didn't name the 'cast; I just stepped in when Meme Girl, uh, left. So I can only guess at her reasoning. But I think she was going for the original definition of a meme.

A meme is a fundamental unit of information—like a gene—that spreads. And the MemeCast gives out small bits of news you might not get anywhere else, and hopefully you spread that info. Yeah, kind of like a virus. Everything is Everything.

On another level, a meme is an idea or practice that's transmitted verbally or by action from one person's mind to another. That meme can be passed down (like from parentals or some other authority) or around from peers and media. So a meme can be a stupid viral pic or vid or some ad catchphrase or tune we're all singing. Or a meme could be something bigger, like Santa Claus or the American Dream.

Or the idea that some ID chips can keep you safe.

The key is that it's something you pass on. Positive or negative. Stupid or sublime.

So I was thinking, if a meme is a like a virus, could you have some sort of epidemic? Sure, I guess. I bet most memes are fairly harmless, like a common cold. But think about a cult, for instance. A cult plants an idea in some schmuck's head, and then that idea consumes him. He gives his all to spreading it. Like a plague.

Whoa, now we're getting too heavy for a friendly little pirate radio 'cast. So let's talk news.

EuroNews is reporting that US troops are pulling out of Syria and other places and heading toward Saudi Arabia. Dozer23 says it's all about the black gold. LtDan45 says he's been reactivated even though he retired last year.

On the home front, we've got thirty-five days left until the election, citizens. The poll numbers for the Patriot Party are on the rise across the country. Mayor Mignon's opponent in the Congressional race, Hermione Wallace, hasn't found any corporate sponsors yet. Nobody wants to bet against TFC, Mignon's biggest backer.

MemeNet update. We hit two hundred fifty active

nodes today in the City of Hamilton. I know that doesn't sound like a lot. But no matter whose law of networking you like, the power of a network is far more than the number of nodes or users; it's all about the connections—and what you do with them.

Next up, I've got an oldie, "Beds are Burning" by Midnight Oil, followed by a new one from our own Wannabes called "In My Dreams."

JEDI MIND TRICK

VELVET

Aiden and Winter had some explaining to do. They usually went to her grandfather's house after school, so the boys and I jetted over to Mr. Yamada's as soon as the last bell rang. Micah had taken off after lunch, and I couldn't blame him. Even *we* had fallen for the whisperings of the chips in our heads.

But the MemeCast should have prevented it. Aiden had engineered this code that was supposed to erase false memories planted by the ID chips—and that code was hidden inside the waves of MemeCast. Somehow.

While we waited, the boys jammed with a ferocity I hadn't heard in them since the rave, actually. Winter had given us the entry code for the back door so we could practice after school. I tried listening to the boys but couldn't sit still. I even attempted the Warped Wall in my skirt and boots.

Fail.

I was attempting what was left of the Curtain Cling when Winter finally came home.

Frantically, I explained to her what had happened to Micah. She and Lina tried an experiment. They turned on the MemeCast signal—I assume the one she'd used on her parents—and played it over the speakers in the Sail sculpture.

"Anything?" she asked.

I shook my head. I could still clearly remember the words: *Jonas M. Wallenberg was convicted of inciting a riot and bombing the corporate headquarters of TFC on—*

Spike and the boys nodded. None of us wanted to say the rest. According to the little voice in our heads, Micah's dad had been executed for treason.

"I was afraid of this," Aiden said glumly as he dropped into the conversation. I hadn't noticed him come in. "TFC patched the security hole in their app. They must have downloaded new firmware without Nomura knowing about it."

"Does that mean they're on to us?"

"Maybe. Firmware and software get updated all the time. Something in the new version may have fixed the vulnerability we were able to exploit."

"English, please," I demanded.

"Maybe it's just a coincidence. They fixed another

problem or installed a new feature that closed off the chip to our signal."

I didn't like how glib he was about it all, as if it was just some technical problem to be solved—instead of Micah's life. "A happy accident?" *Great*. "So we're screwed?"

"No, we've been working on something else at Nomura." He had that gleam back in his eyes. Then Aiden explained how he—along with his aunt and uncle, Winter's parents—had been working on a jailbroken version of the chip. Translation: they'd divorced the regular ID part of the chip from the TFC-controlled part. Aiden had been doing it as part of his "internship" on the down-low. The chip had all the functions of the real deal—identification, communication, money—but the TFC apps (including the secret ones) wouldn't run on it.

"Sounds easier than it was, especially since Nomura designed the chips; but TFC has their fingers in everything. And we want to be able to swap out the chip without alerting TFC. That's the tricky part." Aiden looked worried. "And we can't do that yet."

"Great," Spike said, offering up his head to Aiden. "Pop these puppies out and give us new ones."

"We're working on it." Aiden shifted uneasily. "Soon, I hope."

"So we just have to suck it up?" I asked. I was really tired of sucking it up. The nightmares. The voices. Dad having to go back. Mom and I on our own. The whole shitty deal. Somebody else needed to suck it up for once.

"For now," he said, standing there in his expensive khakis and swank loafers.

Easy for you to say. You don't have this thing whispering lies about your friends. You're not wondering if these whispers are your thoughts or fears. You're really not sucking up anything at all.

I took Spike's hand in mine.

"Walk me home," I whispered.

DIVING INTO THE MEME POOL

MICAH

I cut school the rest of the week and worked on sketch after sketch. That weekend Nora and I turned my coffin doodles into the first issue of *Memento* 2.0. This time, we didn't do a paper copy; we put it on the MemeNet. Aiden created a forum just for the comic—old and new issues. The MemeCast and various bands—including the Wannabes—all had their own forums, too. There were several other forums. They had names like MLSG, Mt. Zion, the Oracle, and the Hour Exchange. I wasn't sure what most of them were. In all of them, people could comment and start conversations on the topic.

The first issue showed exactly what I'd witnessed, from the funeral procession to the teargassing to the cops telling me to run. I put in all the coffin names I could remember, including Jonas W.

At first people had been reluctant to post on the MemeNet for fear of black vans and helicopters swooping down on them. But as soon as we put up this issue of *Memento*, the floodgates opened.

Dozens of people replied. Most of them with unsurprised shock-horror. Some folks reported their loved one had been at the protest and had disappeared. Others commented on the names on the coffins—including Jonas W's.

I poured over these posts for clues. Yes, it was Jonas Wallenberg, my father. Starcity27 said JW was a terrorist. Hippieck73 said that was a lie perpetuated by the Man. Catcall902 said he was a peace activist. Anon78 wrote she'd seen him at MLSG meetings long ago. Anon943 said he'd been in the army. Ant89 said he'd been a suit at TFC. Still another Anon (19) posted that he'd disappeared after the riot fifteen years ago. Others said he'd died in Detention or fled to Argentina or Australia or some other A country.

Was Dad all of these things? None? Something in between? I was even more confused than when I started. So I headed to Nora's place (well, her mom's apartment) and waited for her to come home for the weekend.

Her mom was busy with a client, so I just parked my butt in the lobby and sketched. I checked the *Memento* board a couple of times. (Mrs. James was definitely on the MemeNet.)

I had one more message. AnythingGrl1. *I've got the plot for your next issue. Call me. V.*

19.0

THE BEGINNING OF ENOUGH

VELVET

I told Micah to meet me at the garden. I practically wore a groove in the bamboo walk as I paced back and forth, my boots thudding roughly in time with the music Winter had blaring out of the sail-things. She and Lina were in their usual spot—the workshop—building antennae, routers, and the occasional robot. They are the perfect pair.

The boys were practicing under the Spider Climb on the Sasuke course. With Mr. Yamada's permission, Aiden and the boys had built a tiny recording booth under the obstacle.

Finally, Micah rolled in the back way on his skateboard, messenger bag slung over his shoulder. "What's the deal?"

I stomped up to him. I was so angry—not at him—I

didn't know where to start. "Your comic—" was all I could sputter out.

"What's wrong with it?"

"Nothing!" I almost screamed. I took in a deep breath. "After I saw you at your place that day, I walked home past—" The image of the kid, the smoke, the cops crowded the words out of my brain. I took another deep breath and plunged my shaking hand into my pocket. "—where the TFC had just blown up. The cops were already there, pulling people out—and I stepped into one of those stupid coffin-things." I shuddered without meaning to.

"I'm sorry, V. That must have been rough." Micah stared at me, not quite getting the connection I was trying to make.

I tried again. "I was a block away when I felt the rumble, and by the time I got there, a few seconds later, the cops were already pulling out people. Like the cops—"

"Knew it was going to happen," Micah said slowly. "Or do you mean—"

I nodded. It had been bugging me. There was zero time between the explosion and the cops getting there. In Micah's cartoon, the cops—and the black vans—had been there earlier to bust up the protest. Micah hadn't stuck around to see the aftermath. Maybe the cops or the black van people did something. I'd read the earlier *Memento*s posted on the MemeNet. The black vans always seemed to be in the vicinity of shit that blew up. And the black vans worked for TFC.

"What if TFC blew up one of its own clinics?" I asked.

"And they blamed it on the protestors." Micah sank down onto the edge of the walkway, his head resting on his hands. Just for a moment. Then he slowly pulled out his sketch pad and pens. "Tell me exactly what you saw."

That was the second issue of *Memento* 2.0—and the beginning of a song called "Enough."

THE GOOD DAUGHTER

NORA

Since it was Columbus Day, I didn't have school. But over breakfast Dad casually announced we were hosting a dinner party tonight. A very private, very important soiree having to do with next month's election. "The caterers will take care of everything," he explained. "I just need you there, looking like the good daughter you are."

Bergen's sent over new dresses and shoes for me to try on. Dad said I could only pick one of each, but if this evening went well, I could have a whole new winter wardrobe. And more.

I didn't really care about the clothes. Much. I picked out a pale pink halter-style cocktail dress with matching sandals.

The caterers took over the penthouse with minimal

supervision from me. I just hid in my room, watching 'casts (*Under the Dome* and the historical one, *Regency House*) until it was time to get dressed. I ignored all the newsy interruptions about food shortages, blackouts, and bank failures—as well as the forty-seven Patriot Party ads. I did text Micah once to tell him what I was doing. His response was that it beat lugging boxes of Spam. Maybe. He was working a few hours a week at the food bank where he'd done his community service.

Dad nodded approvingly at my attire and at the caterer's spread in the kitchen.

"You can help the waiters bring out trays," he told me.

I groaned inwardly, but on the outside I plastered on a glossy smile.

The Slaytons were the first to arrive. Mr. Slayton used to work for Dad at Soft Target, but Tom said his dad now worked for Mrs. Slayton. Tom's mom, Rachael Constantine, had gotten a huge promotion at Tyrell Energy Corporation. Vice president of Exploration.

"If we'd known this was a family affair, we'd have brought Tom," she said coolly. Tom's mother did not like me, especially since I'd broken up with her baby boy after the Twinkie Factory rave.

Some guy from Hakita Electronics and a few TFC execs joined the party over the next half hour or so. I smiled and nodded politely whenever Dad introduced me. I carried trays of crab cakes, thinly sliced filet mignon, lobster-stuffed shrimp, and asparagus wrapped in bacon. Then

I retreated to the kitchen to sip diet soda and nibble on carrot sticks and little quiches until I was needed or missed.

Around ten, another guest and her entourage showed up. It was Tyra Foster-Caine, I heard one of the caterers whisper. She was TFC herself.

"Nora," Dad called.

I grabbed a dessert tray filled with minicheesecakes and worked my way across the room—and many conversations. None of them noticed me. They just reached for a chocolate or almond morsel and kept on talking.

"Cheesecake?"

". . . Patriot Party is a bunch of rubes—but very useful . . ."

". . . the key is getting Mignon in, though. Without him . . ."

"And the Europeans are waiting to see how he does . . ."

"Dessert?"

"The country can't afford for the terror bubble to pop yet."

". . . not until we've secured more reserves."

"We can trust Hakita. They've got oil interests, too. . . ."

"Cheesecake?"

"I can't leave her here with her mother, and I may be traveling quite a bit with this new office. . . ."

I looked up at this voice. Dad was talking to Ms. Foster-Caine, CEO of TFC.

"There are some excellent international schools in Hamburg, or you could send her to boarding school in Munich or even Switzerland. My children love Bern," she said.

Hamburg? I bumped into her with the tray.

"Nora," Dad said sharply. The ice clinked in his glass.

Mrs. Slayton rolled her eyes at me. Ms. Foster-Caine looked at me expectantly.

"I'm sorry, ma'am," I said to her.

"Ms. Caine, this is my daughter, Nora."

"Dad, are we moving?" I couldn't help asking.

"Princess, we'll talk about this later."

I hesitated, though he clearly wanted me to evaporate. "Later," he said more curtly and walked the TFC chairman to the patio.

Stunned, I carried the tray back to the kitchen—despite the Slaytons calling for cheesecake. I set the tray down on the kitchen counter hard, harder than I had intended.

Someone grabbed my arm from behind. "You will not embarrass me, young lady," Dad whispered as he twisted my wrist so that I faced him.

"Dad, you're hurting—" I suppressed a yelp. It felt like my wrist was caught in a door or a trap. The caterers turned away. I looked up into his eyes, and I didn't know my dad anymore. It was the beer bottle look times ten.

"You have no idea how important this evening is. My business depends on those people trusting me. And you," he said, his grip tightening on my already throbbing wrist.

I bit my lip to keep myself from crying. "Go to your room before you disappoint me any further."

He let go, and I ran to my bedroom and locked the door.

I slumped against my bed, in my party dress, cradling my arm for a while. I was too shocked and scared to cry.

I looked up Hamburg on my mobile. Germany. Dad was moving us to Germany.

Mom. Micah. I'd never see them again.

That's when I did start to cry.

I was still lying in bed with my party dress on when the alarm went off in the morning.

Dad left a note and a little blue box in the kitchen. The note said simply: *I'm so sorry I lost my temper, Princess.* Inside the box was a new charm for my bracelet: a tiny suitcase with the globe on it. *I want to give you the world,* Dad had scribbled inside the lid of the jewelry box.

21.0

COMING HOME

VELVET

Early in the morning was the hardest time to keep it together. The dreams of the kid in the lime green shirt and of my dad in a paper coffin burst into my sleep in the wee hours. I tossed and turned, trying to get back to sleep, but it wasn't any use. I had to get up at six a.m., anyway, so I could walk to school.

So I pulled on my clothes, made a pot of coffee, grabbed my notebook (and smokes), and headed into the backyard. I sank into the rickety old Adirondack chair wedged under the Japanese maple strewn with fairy lights—and began to write.

The dogs kept me company, especially the big black one, Bridget. Mom told me she was the Black Dog at Black Dog Salvage. Mrs. Shaw couldn't keep her because the TFC apartment didn't allow big dogs. Bridget, aptly named after the Celtic goddess of poetry, lay at my feet snoring as lightly as a ninety-pound rug can.

My insomnia had been quite productive for my song writing. Not so much for school or work. I'd nodded off in trig class more than once this week. Mrs. Huxley, my boss at the vintage store, almost caught me dozing over inventory.

This morning, I was deep into the writing and on my second cup of coffee when Mom wandered into the yard. Usually, she feeds the dogs and then heads over to the community garden about the time I leave for school. Sometimes she'd walk me as far as the bridge. It wasn't daylight yet.

She handed me a bowl of fruit and a fresh-baked biscuit. I hadn't noticed her rattling around in the kitchen.

"You need to eat—not smoke—your breakfast, honey." She scratched behind Bridget's ear and offered her a bite of her own biscuit. She sounded tired and far away—more so than usual.

"Anne Marie." She looked at me all of a sudden. "Velvet, your dad's coming home," she blurted out.

"That's fantastic!" I said, genuinely excited. He hadn't been home on leave since last Christmas. Then I saw the look on her face. Her eyes were bloodshot and her face was drawn. Images of paper coffins flashed by my eyes. "Is he okay?" I could feel the panic welling up inside me like vomit. My hands started shaking again.

"Yes, honey. He's okay. He is wounded, but it's just his leg. Shrapnel. He'll be fine." She reached for me, but I pulled back.

"Promise?" I gulped out, almost in tears. Mom nodded her head, barely holding back her own. We both tried not to cry but failed miserably.

"When?"

"Next Thursday."

Our sacrifices keep them safe.

Damn chip. I knew it was the chip whispering not-so-sweet nothings in my brain, but I couldn't help wondering if there was a connection between my songs (or even the rave) and what happened to Dad. TFC certainly bitch-slapped Micah with the implanted memory of his dad—which was still hard to remember was NOT true.

I was too tired to come up with some pithy addition to the *Book of Velvet* other than this: Aiden better hurry the hell up.

I decided to skip school and help Mom in the garden and get ready for Dad. She didn't object.

ONE DAD PROBLEM TOO MANY

NORA

"They just keep coming in," Micah said.

He spread out sheets of paper on Mom's coffee table. Winter had printed out the Jonas Lives forum messages for him. He read a couple to me. I nodded politely but had a hard time focusing on them because I was thinking about my own father. My wrist still hurt where he'd grabbed me earlier this week. And I knew in my gut he'd lose his temper again. And again. Just like he had with Mom. And now he was possibly taking me to Germany. I'd truly never get to see Mom again—or Micah, for that matter. The reasonable part of my non-glossy brain said I'd be eighteen in a few years and could do what I wanted then. But that was so far away. I pulled my long sleeves down even farther.

Micah was looking at me as if expecting an answer.

"I'm sorry." I shook my head. "What did you say?"

"Are you okay?" He slid closer to me on the couch.

"Let's solve your dad problem first." I gave him a light kiss on the cheek. I wasn't quite ready to face mine yet, even if my wrist was still throbbing.

Micah repeated his question. "There are so many stories. How do we know what's true and what's not?"

"Some have to be true," I said. According to the underground rumor mill, Jonas W. had been army, TFC, and protestor. Most said he was an activist of some kind, which meant he'd probably gotten arrested or sent to Detention when we were little. That was when my mom started defending "those people" as Dad called them. "Maybe we should ask my mom."

Micah blinked at me behind his smudged glasses.

"She might have defended him." Mom had represented Winter's parents once upon a time.

"Worth a shot." Micah shrugged.

I had to admit I didn't hold out much hope, either. With her many trips to TFC, Mom had wiped her brain of most of her old cases, but she might have some inkling of who Jonas was.

The elevator shimmied as we descended to the ground floor. *Did TFC look at all the memories?* I wondered. She'd erased them to protect her clients. Had she hurt them instead? I shook off the thought.

Mom was on her mobile with a client so we waited on

the old dining chairs in her little waiting room. I watched Micah fidget until he couldn't stand it. He pulled out his sketch pad. His pencil started flying over the page, and he visibly relaxed.

I felt an overwhelming urge to kiss him then, but of course Mom stuck her head out just at that moment.

"We need your help," I told her as she sat us down like regular clients in her office. "Micah wants to know what happened to his dad." I let him fill in the rest. He told her everything he'd told me: everything his mom or Mr. Yamada or the people on the boards mentioned about Jonas W.

When he was done, Mom nodded thoughtfully. "I do remember hearing about a Jonas Wallenberg being active in an anti-TFC movement twelve to fifteen years ago." Mom looked from me to him. "But I'm not sure what you want me to do. I'm not a detective."

"Was he one of your clients maybe?" I asked, though I knew the answer.

"I honestly don't remember." That knowledge was another thing in TFC records.

"Thanks, anyway, Mrs. J." Micah stood up, the disappointment dripping off him. I should have warned him. I reached out my hand to his. Mom was looking at us both with a strange smile on her face.

"But I did keep my records."

23.0

UNPLUGGED

VELVET

It was a broiling hot day for October. I'd put on my vintage black Misfits T-shirt and biker boots, hoping it would make me feel tough. I leaned against the bike rack outside Sasuke Ink, waiting for Winter to come hold my hand.

She'd texted last night to say "it" was ready. I knew exactly what she meant. "It" was the replacement chip Aiden and her mom had been working on. I was dying to get this thing out of my skull, but the thought of having things—no matter how tiny—taken out and then put back in my body made me feel weak in the knees. Yes, I was being a wuss.

Aiden walked up the sidewalk with two iced coffees. He handed me one. Black. Exactly how I would've ordered it. I peered around him to see if Winter was following.

"She's not coming," Aiden said.

Crap. I took a deep slurp of my iced coffee.

"She says we should talk," he said, not drinking his. The liquid was creamy and half gone.

"About what?" I snapped, although I knew damn well what. Winter had finally told me why he'd been acting weird around me. Evidently, *he* was what I'd forgotten.

"Maybe about how you've been avoiding me," he said calmly as he settled onto the bike rack next to me. We faced the street together.

"We've seen plenty of each other since school started." I sloshed the ice around in my cup for no real reason.

"Somebody is always with us. Winter. Lina. Micah. Spike. It's never just us." He stared across the street at the boarded-up bodega.

"There is no us," I blurted out and stood to face him. "Not that I remember," I added more gently. Still, it felt crappy to say it out loud.

"Really?" He raised an eyebrow as if unsure whether to believe me. As if I'd lie—to someone other than TFC.

"Should I remember? Did we, you know?" Spike and I hadn't even done *that* yet.

He shook his head. "No. 'Us' consisted of a date at a junkyard and a kiss. Then things got crazy. Winter went off the deep end. You were planning the rave. We were trying to save the world. You know, stuff."

Relief washed over me. I hadn't cheated on Spike. Other than a kiss, which I did feel bad about. "I remember going to the Rocket Garden—many times. Seeing you there. But no date—or kiss." As I said that I had a lingering impression of the taste of coffee and sugar on my lips. "I'm sorry." It sounded lame even to my ears.

He took a long drink of coffee before he said, "It's okay. You couldn't help what you told them, I guess." He straightened up and threw the cup in the trash can next to the rack. "At least you didn't tell them anything important." He struggled to keep the bitterness out of his voice. Or was it regret? I couldn't tell.

But I wondered if I could've helped it. Did I sacrifice the memory of that kiss—something that obviously meant a lot to him—in order not to give any secrets away? Is that how I really got out of the Big D with my other memories intact? Did I unburden myself of my feelings for Aiden to TFC until they told me to shut up and go home? Did I do it for Spike's sake? Or because I was too big a wuss to make a choice? Did I do the right thing?

I reached for his hand, but he pulled away.

"Ready?" he asked with forced breeziness as he opened the shop door for me. "You're the first non-Nomura to get unplugged. We're calling it 'the special.'" Aiden nodded for me to enter.

I touched the raised disc behind my right ear. The thought of removing the chip was unexpectedly making me want to wimp out. But I had to get rid of this thing.

He'd led me through Mr. Yamada's tattoo shop, past Jet and Mr. Yamada himself as they worked on customers. No one looked up. We passed through a beaded screen under a sign that said PIERCINGS. The booth in the back was scrupulously clean—not that the rest of the shop wasn't—but this area was sterile and antiseptic like a hospital.

A small woman with Winter's X-ray eyes donned a surgical mask as she entered the booth from a back room. She had a white smock over her jeans and T-shirt and white paper booties pulled over her pale pink Firenze pumps.

Aiden introduced us. "This is my aunt Spring, Winter's mom." He flicked a switch that turned on some fan system and a brighter light as well as another switch that didn't appear to do anything. "This helps block the signal to the chip."

"Talk later," Mrs. Nomura said curtly. "We've only got a few minutes." She waved me into the chair.

She swabbed behind my ear as I clutched Aiden's hand. I could feel something cold and metallic press against the spot behind my right ear. I steeled myself but only felt a slight pop. I still jumped a little.

Mrs. Nomura placed the disc on a tray. The thin wafer, no bigger than a contact lens, didn't look so menacing now. Aiden unwrenched himself from my death grip with a murmur of apology. He placed the disk in some contraption, pressed a button, then handed Mrs. N a new chip. "Just transferring your info to the new chip."

Again I felt the cold metal press against my skull. I didn't jump as much this time when it popped into place.

Aiden put the old chip in a disposal marked medical waste, and it burned up in a flash. He flicked the do-nothing switch off.

It was all over in a few seconds. And it had been relatively painless. Yet I could feel the tears welling up.

"Hey, what's the matter?" Aiden brushed a tear from my cheek. Mrs. Nomura excused herself out the back.

I told him about my dad coming home, the dreams, and what I'd seen outside TFC No. 23. He'd actually guessed the last part from the latest issue of *Memento*. I felt better for having told someone everything.

Mr. Yamada stuck his head through the beads. "Everything okay in here?"

I nodded, wiping away my tears, which were quickly ruining my tough chick façade. "Shouldn't I get a piercing or tattoo to cover up for 'the special'?"

"Nah, I'll just tell anyone who asks that I kicked you out for not having parental permission." Mr. Yamada grinned. "Or I could give you a sticker."

No, thanks. So much for the tough chick.

"She does have a good point, Dad," Mrs. Nomura chimed in from the back. "Somebody will get suspicious if a whole bunch of people waltz out of here with nothing to show."

"And it would be cool to have a tattoo or something that symbolized what we're doing," Aiden added. "Kind of a visible meme."

I wasn't so sure we needed to advertise. But I had been wanting a tattoo.

Mr. Yamada nodded thoughtfully. "It would have to be small, simple, and non-obvious."

I stared at the tats on his hands. His whole arm, really. A snake flowed down his right arm with the head ending at his hand. Something like that must have taken forever—and hurt like heck.

Something small—and fast. "What about the tattoo Winter gave herself?"

Mrs. Nomura's eyebrows shot up at that. Had she not noticed the perfect circle on Winter's left hand? She'd shown up at school one day a couple of months ago sporting fresh ink that looked like a calligrapher had done it. She said she'd done it herself to try out a tattoo rig she'd modded for Jet. I could sit still long enough for a circle.

"The perfect circle. It can mean many things," Mr. Yamada picked his words carefully under the glare of his daughter. "Sun. Moon. Protection. Unity. Time. Wholeness."

I could buy that last one. And one quick call to my mom later, I had my first tattoo. On my calf, which Mr. Yamada said was one of the least painful places to get it done.

The perfect circle became "the special" of Sasuke Ink.

NORMALITY IS ALL IT'S CRACKED UP TO BE

VELVET

Thursday finally came. We sprang for a cab to get Dad home from the airport. As I opened the door of the beat-up Chevy Spark, I heard the last strains of the MemeCast. Neo was talking about a blackout in Florida when the cabbie reached her tattooed hand to turn it off. She had a black circle on the back of her hand.

"It's cool," I said, flashing my calf as I got into the front seat.

The 'cast turned into music, and we rode to the airport in happy silence.

Dad limped out of the security area leaning heavily on a metal cane. He was still wearing his desert camo and had his duffel slung over his shoulder. I almost didn't recognize him. He was leaner and older than the Travis Kowalcyk who usually bounded out to scoop me up.

I stuffed my hand in my pocket as he made his way across the lobby. He moved carefully and deliberately, as if he were navigating a mine field. My feet felt rooted in concrete.

"Velvet," Mom urged as she went forward to meet him.

It took me a few seconds—it felt like an eternity—to uproot my feet from their spot on the walkway. Then I was running past Mom.

He'd been wounded before—in Venezuela, I think, or maybe in the early days of the Middle East 2.0—but I'd been too little to understand or remember much.

Dropping his bag, Dad did his best approximation of scooping me up—with one hand firmly on the cane. He smelled like fresh GI issue deodorant, stale airplane air, and peppermint.

He wrapped an arm around Mom, and I grabbed his duffel—with a groan. The weight of it nearly took my arm off. "What have you got in here? A tank?" It somehow made me feel better. He may have been a temporary gimp, but he'd lifted this bag as if it had been a clutch purse. Okay, bad example.

Still, as I watched him lean into his cane to open the cab door for Mom, I couldn't help thinking I had something to do with all this.

Once we got home, Dad was so exhausted he could only make it as far as the couch. Mom shooed the dogs into the backyard and started clearing junk off the counters in the kitchen as if she were actually going to cook something.

That left me the choice of staring at my dad sleeping or my mom cooking. I joined the dogs and sat under my tree.

The sun beat down through the green and gold leaves, bathing me in warmth. I was soon asleep myself. Unfortunately, I dreamed of Dad clicking through a minefield of paper coffins. His cane brushed one lightly and it exploded. That woke my ass up.

By then, Mom actually had a pretty respectable dinner ready. Pasta with fresh tomato sauce and veggies. Garlic bread. Ice tea. Dad was all over it. Mom giggled, watching him eat.

Normal is everything it's cracked up to be. *Book of Velvet*. Chapter 5, Verse 3.

Dad paused halfway through his plate of spaghetti. "Syl, this is fantastic. Did you get all of it from the garden?"

Mom, the queen of bartering, beamed. "The vegetables are. I traded zucchini for the bread, and the pasta is from the food bank."

Dad raised an eyebrow at that last part. He was all for hustling but not for taking handouts.

"You know I volunteer there, and Simon lets me take home a bag of out-of-date stuff every now and then."

That's how she got a lot of the dog food, too. Some

stores donated stuff that was way past its expiration date. The food bank couldn't legally give it to its clients, but Simon—the warehouse manager—turned a blind eye to volunteers taking old dry and canned goods home.

"That's my girl," Dad said with a laugh. "Your mom would make an outstanding quartermaster, V. She can scrounge with the best of them." Then he turned serious. "While I'm home, we need to turn it up a notch on the prep work, Sylvia."

"Soon?" Mom asked.

I hadn't a clue what they were talking about.

"Maybe not right this minute, but it's coming." Dad looked around the kitchen and then glanced upward. "Anyone upstairs?"

Mom shook her head.

"What are you guys talking about?"

"Velvet, honey," Dad said slowly. "One day soon, the shit is going to hit the fan. And your mom has been getting us ready."

I tried to pry more of an explanation from them, but they only muttered something about oil. Mom and Dad spent the rest of the evening talking about storing food, planting their own garden in the back (landlord be damned), and alternative power sources. I threw in that Winter knew how to make solar panels. Dad gave me a thumbs-up on that and added it to the extensive list he was making. He was beginning to remind me of that doomsday prepper 'cast where the crazy guy thinks some super volcano is going to erupt. So he fills his garage with energy bars, shotguns, and chemical toilets.

Later that night I heard Dad yell out something—followed by Mom trying to wake him up. Then I heard him bumping his way to the kitchen. I found him there, slathering a slice of bread with peanut butter and jelly.

"Did I wake you up?" he asked.

"Couldn't sleep anyway." It was true. I made myself some herbal tea, though I knew it wouldn't help.

We sat at the table across from each other, and I watched him wolf down his PB&J. He washed it down with a cold glass of milk.

"Would you ever go to TFC?" I asked him. I knew the answer. At least, I knew what he'd said before, but I thought maybe the years had changed his mind.

"You heard that, huh?" He shook his head. "No, but to be honest I think about it every day."

"What stops you?" I knew they had TFCs on base. The treatment was supposedly developed for servicemen in the first place. The army even gives them Amelioral (the TFC drug) for free, if they want it.

"A buddy of mine swore by Ameliorol, back when TFC first started the clinics. He'd gotten injured in Venezuela and lost about half his squad in the action, too. He got a medical discharge but couldn't quite hack it in the real world. The treatments seemed to pull him out of his tail-spin. He got his shit together for several years, even went to work for the company, had a kid, big house, the works. I lost touch with him, since I was still in the service and he was a successful civilian. Then out of the blue he wrote me to warn me never to take the treatments. He claimed they didn't work like the company said they did."

Dad stopped to take a long swallow. He looked deeply sad, thinking about his friend. I could guess what happened. "Anyway, I figure it's better to deal with stuff as it comes up. I'm not knocking it for some, mind you. But in combat, I need to remember the mistakes that cost lives. You know? I need to remember the faces of those who died. Keeps me sharp."

We were quiet for a long second.

"But how do you deal? When you're not in combat, that is." If Dad could cope with what he'd seen, I could suck it up, too.

"That, darling, is the million-dollar question." He rose and kissed me on the cheek. "You keep writing those songs, Velvet Kowalcyk," he whispered in my ear. He winked at me as he headed back toward the bedroom. "It's a start."

I wrote that down in my notebook.

THE HUMAN ELEMENT

Okay, citizens. Neo here again. I might wax all philosophical about freeing the information or opening doors and all that. But if I'm honest with myself (which I rarely am), what I really know about is scamming people. I'm a hacker, but some might call my coding skills skid-level or noobish. I'm far better at hacking social situations IRL. In real life. (Except when it comes to certain females lately. But that's a whole different thing.)

The human element is the weakest part of any system.

For instance, let's say I wanted to get your password at work. I could try all sorts of techie tactics—brute force password generators, keyloggers, etc. But the easiest way is to have you give it to me.

You'd never do that, right?

What if someone from Tech Support called and said your system was infected with a worm that was going to destroy your store's payroll (or inventory or whatever) database. Tech Support Guy (aka me) tells you all the terrible things that'll happen if you don't act fast. Bottom line: your job will be toast if this isn't fixed stat. So I begin walking you through how to fix it, but the screens keep getting more and more technical and complicated. I can sense you're frustrated and a little scared, so I magnanimously offer to fix it for you remotely. You just have to give me your password. By then, you're ready to give me your firstborn child, and you hand over the keys gladly. And I'm your savior—and now I can do what I want. (And you probably do lose your job.)

But you know what works even better? Let's say I create the problem in the first place—and then I'm the one who cleans it up.

(Don't try this at home, folks.)

Either way, the idea is to make the mark feel small and inadequate (like a child, if you must), and then you sweep in like the parent figure to save the day. The mark feels grateful and relieved.

Don't think hackers are the only ones who use this tactic. Salesmen play this game all the time. So do doctors, mechanics, economists, media pundits, and politicians.

In the news, sources say there's rioting in the Saudi capital, Riyad, and several other cities. And no, it's not a Coalition takeover but a popular uprising. My European connection also tells me a lot of transatlantic flights have been canceled, and people in some places in Eastern Europe are lining up for food and oil, old-Soviet style.

THE ROAD TO ZION

MICAH

Mrs. James kept paper records of her clients' cases in an old storage facility on the edge of town. Just in case.

"I haven't been there since I stopped practicing." She explained that she'd paid cash for a lifetime locker and put it under a fake name.

"Does Dad know?" Nora asked in a hushed whisper.

Mrs. J shook her head. "You're the only two people I've ever told." She retrieved an old key from her safe and pressed it into Nora's hand. "And let's keep it like that."

"We won't tell," Nora said defensively.

"I know. Just be careful," her mom said.

I knew what she meant even if Nora didn't. We shouldn't take Nora's car service, or a taxi, or anything traceable. We'd be hoofing it or taking a bike, I told her as we walked toward the river.

I knew where the place was, sort of. We could ride out the old greenway along the river. The thin ribbon of tarmac had never gotten finished years ago, so the bike path just sort of stopped after you crossed this bridge across the river. It was a bridge to nowheresville, since the park on the other side never got built. Mt. Zion Self Storage was on that side of the river, down along the railroad tracks. You could get to it by car or bus if you went the long way.

The greenway along the river had become the unofficial byway to get around. We took the 72 bus to Thirteenth Street. Then we walked a block to the U-cycle shop wedged under the overpass near the entrance to Thomas Park. I picked out two faded red bikes left in the slots. Nora hesitated before jumping on hers—but just for a second or two.

"People used to do this for fun," I said to her as we pedaled toward the park.

"We have bike trails in LP, but . . ." She trailed off as we passed a few tents along the overgrown part of the greenway. I could guess she was going to say something like "but we don't have people living on the trails."

Most of the greenway was lined with garden plots and temporary stalls for bartering vegetables, crafts, clothes, and other junk. There was even an "official" hour-exchange booth where you could keep track of your barters. "If you work two hours cutting lawns for person X, you might trade it for a few loaves of bread or a shirt from somebody else on the exchange," I explained to Nora, even though she didn't really ask.

"Skaterboy," Mr. Kim called out from his stall.

I motioned for Nora to pull over. Mr. Kim held out two iced ciders.

"Oracle's orders." Mr. Kim pressed a cup into Nora's hand. I didn't need to be asked twice. "Skaterboy and his friends drink free. Come back later when she has a fresh batch of muffins." Mr. Kim nodded toward the next stall over. Mt. Zion Baked Goods was scrawled on an old blackboard, with the specials listed below in colored chalk. "She ran out early this morning."

I downed the fresh apple goodness gratefully—and so did Nora after a few sniffs. Then we thanked Mr. Kim and took off again.

"What was that about? Skaterboy?"

"He's always offering me freebies—a drink, a bowl of noodles, or something from the neighboring stalls—ever since I dropped a load of modded mobiles and hotspots here. At the request of someone calling herself the quote-unquote Oracle. That's her MemeNet handle. Mine's Skaterboy."

"The MemeNet's down here?" Nora asked with a certain rich-girl surprise in her voice.

"Yep. While you were putting nodes behind compound

gates, I was down here." I cycled ahead. This was where the MemeNet was needed. The Hour Exchange used it for keeping track of trades. People communicated with each other. They even organized a bike patrol after dark.

Other people on bikes passed by us. A few had suits on, but mostly our fellow U-cyclers wore uniforms—from hotels, restaurants, garages, delivery services, etc.

Nora caught up with me. "I didn't mean it that way."

Kids played ball in the ankle-high grass and swung on creaking swings. The leaves were turning brilliant oranges and reds. We passed a guy fishing in the quietly burbling river. Nora smiled, finally seeming to enjoy the ride.

We came to the rusted metal and wood bridge to nowhere. The greenway stopped on the other side.

"Are you sure it's safe?"

I shrugged. The wood seemed intact, but it had been patched here and there with boards of different colors and thicknesses.

We walked our bikes over just to be sure. The bridge creaked but held. Then we picked our way down a dirt path along the railroad tracks toward the massive storage facility.

From the side, it looked like an endless wall of garages. All rust-orange doors rolled down and presumably locked. A chain-link fence encircled the whole place, which must have been the size of a football field.

We walked our bikes around to the front. An old falling-down church sat at the corner of Nineteenth Street and the parking lot. The little placard by the church said MT. ZION *AME*.

The storage place wasn't open. The "security gate" was down across the parking lot entrance, but the painted two-by-four posed no challenge to anyone on foot or bike. The front windows of the tiny square brick building marked OFFICE were boarded up, and one of the sheets of plywood had *Memento* spray-painted in red across it. Another chain-link fence circled the storage units, the first row of which you could easily see through. The faded orange metal door of each unit was clearly shut and locked in place. The access gate next to the office was also heavily chained and padlocked.

"We'll have to climb the fence," Nora said, much to my surprise.

I climbed up without replying, pausing at the top to help her if she needed it. She leaned her bike carefully against the building.

"I got this," she said as she pulled herself to the top.

I caught a strange, familiar whiff of something as I dropped lightly to the concrete pad. Nora climbed carefully down the links until her feet were on terra firma.

"What number are we looking for?" I asked Nora quietly.

"Two twenty-seven."

The first row of lockers—the ones facing the front— seemed okay. A little rusty and faded, but all locked tightly. However, as we wound our way into the maze-like facility, we passed opened doors, empty lockers, lockers with junk neatly sorted into piles, some with charred piles of stuff.

"I've got a bad feeling about this," I whispered.

Nora nodded.

We still pressed forward. As we rounded another corner, I could hear laughter. There was a hand-painted sign on the side of an empty locker: VILLAGE SWAP MEET, TUESDAY 8 A.M. The sign looked new.

"Hey, you! What are you doing here?" a gruff—yet cracking—voice called from behind us. Nora visibly jumped at the sound. I could hear the smack of baseball bat against flesh. I pushed Nora behind me, though she resisted, as we turned around.

A tall, redheaded, and sunburned kid, maybe nineteen, stood there, bat held mid-palm smack. "Micah?" he asked.

It was Jimmy Peterson, the oldest of the Peterson kids. Our families had lived in Black Dog Village. His mom, Melinda, helped Mrs. Brooks bake bread.

That's what I smelled. Wood smoke. Rosemary. Bread.

"Is Mrs. B here, too?" I felt happier than I had in days. This week wouldn't totally suck. A bell went off in my thick skull. Mt. Zion Bakery. Duh.

Jimmy laughed and slung the bat over his shoulder. "Come with me."

We followed him around a few more turns, past different-sized storage units, most in some state of pilferage.

Nora had noticed it, too. Then the rows opened up into a large space, a courtyard of sorts, ringed by rows of units. In that courtyard, the younger Peterson kids were playing soccer with a few others I didn't recognize. A canopy had been strung across the courtyard to block the sun and rain—and prying eyes in the sky. A hodgepodge of chairs sat around several pushed-together tables in the center of the square. All of the storage units were open—and looked well lived in. Cots. Mattresses. Dressers. Even lights. It lacked the charm of Black Dog Village, but it was a place to live.

"Boy, what the heck are you doing here?" Mrs. B steamed up to me.

I'd never been so happy to see anyone. And obviously she'd missed me. She wrapped me in a bear hug.

"This is Nora," I said after Mrs. B released me—and I caught my breath.

"Nora James." Mrs. B nodded. "Good to see you, too."

Of course, Mrs. B still had her memories.

And her oven. She fed us fresh carrot cake and mint tea before she let us talk. The rest of the new village—the Petersons and everyone else—gathered around the tables to listen.

Mrs. B told us they'd come here a week or so after Black Dog Village was raided. The Petersons had a unit here, but the place had gone bankrupt years ago.

"You shouldn't have come looking for me, young man," she said, suddenly stern.

I hesitated. Why should she mind? Did she think I'd blow their cover?

"We didn't," Nora said it for me. I was a little ashamed to admit it. Nora explained what we were looking for—but not why.

Number 227 was open and partially empty. Some of the boxes had spilled onto the floor, and some were moldy.

Nora looked at Mrs. B accusingly.

"Child, some of these units were damaged long before we got here. River flooding. Break-ins. Deadbeat auctions."

"We can look through what's left and maybe find a clue." Nora didn't seem like she was buying it, and my hopes weren't too high, either.

It was like searching though a moldy haystack. We found a few files on the Nomuras—Spring and Brian. A few other names we didn't recognize. But no Wallenberg.

I was ready to admit defeat. I sank down on the concrete slab outside Mrs. James's unit. Nora put her arm around me.

"Now are you going to tell me what you're really looking for?" Mrs. B asked, towering over us.

I told her. I always told her everything.

"Your father was not a terrorist," she said simply.

"Did you know him?" I asked, looking up into her always startling gray eyes.

"I taught him in high school—him and that best friend of his. They joined the army together. He met your mom in the army, too. Venezuela, I think. I didn't see him again until many, many years later. He spoke at a rally protesting the new TFC clinics. Then he disappeared. I tried to keep an eye on your mother and you, even after I lost my job. Your mama never talked about it."

It was a lot to take in. Dad had been in the army and then got in trouble for protesting TFC.

"Who was his best friend?" Nora asked out of the blue.

"Travis Kowalcyk."

Nora had a knack for asking the right question at the right time.

26.0

CAN'T ALWAYS GET WHAT YOU WANT

VELVET

Spike sank into the tattered green-and-white lawn chair in my backyard and peeled the bandage up just a bit to peek at the perfect circle tattoo on his wrist. He quickly covered it back up and took a deep breath.

"Still a little bloody?" I asked. Spike did not like blood. Or needles. I'd had to distract him through the whole process by quizzing him on music trivia.

"Babe, I wish you'd called me to go with *you*," he said, still irritated.

We'd already had this conversation. On the phone. On the way to Mr. Yamada's shop. And on the way back. I told him everything that happened and everything Aiden said. Spike wasn't going to let it alone until he got the answer he was looking for.

I leaned back in my rickety Adirondack chair, under the lone tree in our yard, with a bowl of fresh-picked green beans in my lap. I tore off the ends of a bean and pulled its string free. I snapped the bean into three pieces and tossed it back into the bowl. The end bits I threw to the rabbity little dachshund rolling around in the leaves at Spike's feet. None of the other dogs liked raw beans. I fell into a soothing rhythm—*snap*, string, toss—before answering Spike's unasked question.

"There is nothing between Aiden and me. He said it was just a trip to the junkyard—"

"And a kiss, which you conveniently don't remember." Spike didn't look at me. He got his guitar out of its beat-up case and concentrated on tuning. He was trying so hard not to let the hurt show.

"I remember the important things," I said.

Spike shrugged.

"I remember the first time *you* kissed me." I put the bowl aside and crouched at his feet. I had to push the weiner dog out of my way, but I forced Spike to look me in the eye. "You walked me home on the last day of school. We'd missed the stupid bus for some reason, and I was upset because Winter had been hospitalized. Or so I thought."

"Boy, they were messing with our minds even then," he said, striking an off-note on his Gibson. We'd also been pissed because we thought Micah had been sent to juvie.

"You walked me all the way to my place, pestering me with your damn music trivia."

That got him to smile. "Yeah, I think we argued over who was the better songwriter: Dylan or Bono."

"We did, and you're still wrong." I grinned. "But it was exactly what I needed."

Somewhere around Market Street he'd taken my hand. By the time we'd gotten to my house, his arm was around my waist—and we were a couple. At my fence, he'd brought his hand up to my cheek. "They'll be okay, V," he'd said. Then he'd planted a soft but firm kiss on my lips. He tasted like cinnamon gum. And I'd kissed him back. "It'll be an epic summer," he'd said as I walked into the house. And at that moment, I thought he'd be right.

"I remember that kiss, too." He put down his guitar and looked me square in the eye. "And your ass looked fine walking away in those jeans. Still does."

I laughed. "Crude but effective," I said. Spike had a knack for saying the exactly right "wrong thing" at the right time. He made me feel wanted.

I pulled his head toward mine and kissed him. He still tasted like cinnamon.

Mom tapped at the window. "Damn," Spike whispered as we parted.

"Now can we work on some songs?" I asked as I settled back into my chair with the green beans.

"If your folks weren't watching us from the kitchen . . ."

he said as he adjusted himself under the cover of the guitar.

"Put that energy into figuring out a melody for this." I handed him my lyric notebook and opened it to a song I was calling "Enough."

"Okay, okay . . . too bad we don't have a gig to play it at." He balanced the book on his knee and strummed out several variations on his guitar while I fell back into green bean mode. The little dog—who I was going to start calling Beanie—curled up between Spike's feet. Spike crooned the words softly with each new chord structure he tried.

Not bad, I thought as I watched him lose himself in the music. Not freaking bad at all.

In the immortal words of Mick Jagger, sometimes you get what you need. *Book of Velvet*. Chapter 19, Verse 3.

And maybe what we needed was a gig. An epic one.

27.0

THE TALE OF TANK AND DOZER

MICAH

Nora was a good sport. First she'd gone to a storage-facility-turned-homeless-camp with me, and now she was tagging along to confront Velvet's dad in the mostly boarded-up end of the West End. (I confess. I'm a wuss. I waited until she could go with me.) Los Palamos, with its security gates, green lawns, and perfect houses, was more her kind of place.

She'd grabbed my hand as we boarded the 72 bus near her mother's place.

As we crawled through downtown past another ID check barrier, Nora watched the ads flicker across her seat screen. Mine were all about the news. Elections. Terrorists. Oil. War. The usual.

I stared out the window trying not to think about what Mr. Kowalcyk might tell me.

The bus made a stop across from the padlocked ruins of Black Dog Salvage. The wall around the place had been tagged with graffiti that hurt to see. Most of it said something about bombs or terrorists. That's the excuse the city had used to close the place down—someone had found bomb-making materials there. It was bullshit. Just like my dad being a terrorist was bullshit. BDV had been my safe place, the place where everything made sense.

Nora took my hand as we pulled away from the stop. I wondered if I'd taken her here before. It was still weird not to remember how we'd gotten together in the first place.

The bus turned left on Thirteenth Street toward rows of boarded-up houses. When we got to Jackson Avenue, I pulled the old-fashioned cord to stop the bus.

Nora death-gripped my hand as we got off. Many of the houses in this part of the West End had symbols graffitied on the front doors.

"That just marks if a squat is taken," I explained. "But not all the houses are squats. The Kowalcyks rent theirs," I added, not wanting to totally freak Nora out.

I watched her study the houses as we walked by. Some houses were once-beautiful, dilapidated giants that the owners obviously had to walk away from. We passed a faded and peeling pink house with turrets. A skinny yellow farmhouse-looking place with a rotting porch. A white box of a house with sagging black shutters. A few houses were still being cared for, like the nicely painted blue Victorian with white rocking chairs and potted flowers on the front porch.

In my Black Dog days, I'd helped Mr. Shaw salvage parts from some of these houses. Fireplace mantels. Stained-glass windows. Banisters. Clawfoot tubs. The owners couldn't sell the places, so they tried to get some money out of them. Once upon a time, Mr. Shaw said there was good money in architectural salvage. Folks came to him to get authentic pieces for the renovation of their old houses. Now everyone with that kind of money had moved to a compound, leaving the rest of us high and dry outside the gates.

"That's Velvet's," I said, pointing to a pale yellow Victorian with a slightly weathered picket fence out front. Tomato plants hung from baskets over the porch. And only the third floor was boarded up. Nora relaxed and released her grip on my hand.

When I knocked, a chorus of barks answered. Nora jumped. I forgot to tell her about the Kowalcyk pack. "Velvet's mom rescues dogs. She takes in more than she gives away."

And a half-dozen dogs of all sizes spilled out of the front door when a wiry, short-haired man opened it. Mr. Kowalcyk. I'd only seen him a few times when I was younger. He was hardly ever home on leave. He leaned on his cane as he stared at me. But before he could say anything, a black blur knocked me on my butt.

"Bridget!" I hugged the black dog of Black Dog Salvage and the former guardian of Black Dog Village.

"Guess she knows you, Micah." Mr. Kowalcyk helped me to my feet.

Bridget sniffed Nora once and ran back into the house.

"And you, too," I told her. I guess I *had* taken Nora to BDV.

"Velvet's out back," Mrs. Kowalcyk called from the kitchen as Mr. K corralled the other dogs back into the house. He hobbled to the table in the kitchen, where he had parts of some kind of motor laid out. I had to check it out. He was a mechanic of some kind in the army. "It's for a generator," Mr. Kowalcyk explained. "I'm trying to adapt this one to run on bio-fuel, which we have plenty of." He eyed the pack of dogs lining up to go out the dog flap.

I laughed, despite being as nervous as hell.

"Travis, honey, would you please move that mess so I can start canning the beans?" Mrs. K was washing out dozens of little glass jars in the sink.

Through the window over the sink, I could see Velvet sitting in a lawn chair in the back with a huge bowl of green beans between her feet. She was stringing and snapping them while Spike strummed his guitar. Mrs. K knocked on the window to get their attention.

"We actually came to see you, Mr. Kowalcyk," I said.

"Want me to—" Nora motioned toward the backyard.

I took her hand. "Stay put. This is Nora James, by the way."

Mr. Kowalcyk set down his tools. "Have a seat then." He pulled out a kitchen chair and eased himself into it.

"You knew my dad, right?" I asked.

Mr. K nodded. "You look like him. We were best friends in high school. Even joined the army together." He told us about their first tour in the South American oil fields, Dad getting wounded, and meeting Mom.

Mom had told me how they met. She'd been a nurse in the army, and Dad was one of her patients. But she never said more than that. Now here was somebody who'd known Dad all of his life, and nobody had bothered to tell me. Didn't anybody think I'd want to know?

"Dad, you never told me you and Mr. Wallenberg were friends," Velvet said. I looked up to see Velvet and Spike standing in the kitchen doorway. She gave me a sorry-dude-I-would've-told-you look. And she would have. We'd been tight since third grade.

Mr. Kowalcyk exchanged a look with his wife. She started to say something, but I stopped her.

"Doesn't matter." I was pissed. Somebody should've told me, but right now I only cared about one thing. "What happened to him?" I started pacing, and the words tumbled out before Mr. K could answer. I told Sergeant Travis Kowalcyk all the things I'd heard or read about Jonas Wallenberg. "I don't know what to think, and I can't get a straight answer," I said when I was done.

"Does your mother know you're here?" Velvet's mom asked.

"The boy should know, Sylvia. And maybe Sonia can't tell him."

I stopped pacing.

"Jonas and me lost touch after he left the army," Velvet's dad continued. He explained how my father struggled with PTSD until he tried the new TFC drug. My dad turned his life around and even got a job with the company. "He was wearing suits, and I was still wearing camo."

"Wait a minute. Are you saying my dad worked for TFC?" I sat down with a thud. I had not expected to hear that, not in a million years. My dad was a suit for TFC?

Mr. K nodded. "In the early days, before they went all corporate. TFC used to be a military contractor, running the chow lines and infirmaries and even the oil rigs. Lots of vets went to work for them."

That made me feel only marginally better.

"That was about the time you kids were born, Micah," Mrs. K added. "Jonas and Sonia moved to one of the compounds. And they were both so busy with their jobs. Your mom was head nurse at Los Palamos Hospital. I hardly ever saw either of them. But they did come to Anne Marie's christening."

A compound? That was a lot to process. My dad worked for TFC, and we lived in a compound. I glanced at Nora.

"Was that the last time you talked to him?" she asked Velvet's dad.

"No, maybe a year or two later, Tank told me never to go to one of those TFC clinics."

"Tank?" I asked, confused. My brain was on overload.

"That was your dad's nickname in high school, and it stuck through boot camp and beyond. Mine was Dozer. Wonder why we ended up mechanics and combat engineers?"

Mrs. K brought the conversation back on track. "Your father quit and started organizing protests against TFC. That cost Sonia her job eventually."

"Then the next thing I hear he's . . . gone," Mr. K said sadly.

"Dead?" Nora asked. She voiced the question I couldn't ask. My mouth was unable to form the words.

"I'm not sure exactly what happened. To this day. Your mom never would say. Or maybe couldn't say."

"How do you know he's really dead then?" I demanded. He couldn't be. Jonas Wallenberg couldn't be dead.

"I came home for his funeral," Mr. K said. "I can show you where he's buried."

I numbly followed Mr. Kowalcyk to a small cemetery not too far from the house. Nora tried to take my hand, but I didn't want to be comforted—not yet. The cemetery plots were as overgrown and uncared for as some of the houses in the neighborhood around them. Velvet's dad knelt clumsily and brushed aside the ivy from a tombstone in a particularly overgrown part of the graveyard. The stone just had his name, Jonas M. Wallenberg, and a date.

Now I knew where he was.

Many small stones lined the top of the tombstone. I picked up a rock from the ground and placed it beside them. Nora, Velvet, Spike, and Mr. K did the same.

"Tell me about my dad," I told Mr. Kowalcyk.

"Your dad was a great guy. Funny as hell. Gave a damn. He had all these plans when we were kids. Army. College. Family. A big one. And he always wanted to run for office. Be a congressman or something. He thought he could fix more than tank engines, you know." Mr. K told us more as we walked back. About the division championship game their senior year. He told us about being deployed to Kuwait together. It was like he'd been waiting for someone to ask him about Jonas, about his friend. He started to tell us about a time in Hawaii, but then he reddened and muttered something about "when I'm older." He shook his head and didn't say anything else after that, but I could tell by the little smile that he was remembering and missing Dad.

Nora took my hand in the silence. This time I didn't push it away.

BIRTH OF ANOTHER BRILLIANT IDEA

MICAH

After our little trip to the graveyard, I had another *Memento* rattling around in my head. But it was still a jumble that didn't want to settle down on the paper. Not all the pieces fit together—and I wasn't sure I even had them all.

Was some crank or devoted follower making like Dad was alive to mess with me or push some agenda? Velvet and the guys thought so. Nora hadn't been so sure. "Maybe it's really him," she said as we'd walked home from the bus stop. She voiced the one thing I really wanted to hear but didn't dare believe. And I loved her for it.

I showed Nora the gap(s) in my sketches. "What do you think?" I asked her as she leafed through one of her mom's vintage home magazines.

"Hmm, sorry." She put down the mag and looked at my sketches so far. "I don't know, Micah," she said with a sigh that irritated me.

"What's wrong with you?" I snapped. This was important—to me, at least—and she was someplace else. Then I remembered she'd said something earlier that I'd totally ignored. I'd been so caught up in my long-gone dad that I'd forgotten about her too present one—who was trying to get custody of her.

"How's your dad problem?" I asked, trying to not to sound like the total douche that I was.

She explained what she'd overheard at the party. And the bottom line was that her dad could get sole custody of her and move her to Germany.

First Dad, now Nora. The suckage never stops.

"I thought your mom was fighting it?"

"She is, but—" Nora rubbed her arm.

I understood. She didn't think her mom had a snowball's chance. Action News had been covering the case more and more, but that wouldn't count squat in court.

"You don't get a choice?" Every kid in every 'cast or movie about divorce got to choose what parent he wanted to live with.

"Maybe, but will they listen to me? I need a really good reason. One that I can prove." She tugged down her sleeves. She was wearing a long sleeve T-shirt even though it was eighty degrees out.

"We'll think of something." It was all I could think to say, and I knew how lame it sounded.

Nora shrugged. Then she seemed to come to some sort of decision.

"No, I'm just going to have to fix this situation myself." She hugged herself as she rose. "And maybe I can get you some answers, too."

DELIVERING THE BLUE PILL

AIDEN

Nora wasn't asking for much—just hacking TFC's customer records.

"Give me a few days," I said. I needed to do some recon first. It might even take a week or two, I told her, with midterms coming up and me still working at Nomura. Plus, we were finally beta testing the database hack, with a few people like Lina sporting the virgin fake ID chips. And my mother was coming home soon.

First, a little pretexting. I made a few calls on a burn mobile, pretending to be looking for a job, but really looking for any little door that might crack open. All the hiring, the annoyed voice on the other end told me, was done through an agency—except tech support. I turned on the charm a bit with a sob story about having to quit college to support my ailing mother, and the now-nice woman told me that Speedy Geek handled their computer systems. She even gave me a name and number to talk to.

With a few clicks, I'd sussed out Speedy Geek's procedures and org chart, which were all on the company's woefully unguarded internal network. They did not have remote access to customer systems. That would have been too easy. They mostly just handled plugging in hardware, unjamming printers, and other user-induced problems. But with a little digital dumpster-diving through personnel records, I had some credentials of a tech guy on vacation, Thomas Anderson. Then I fished through the trouble ticket system looking for a good bite.

And there it was, the universe whispered: an installation problem at TFC No. 23. The description said the clinic hadn't reopened yet but was scheduled to do so in a few days, on November 1. They sure rebuilt that place fast. I assigned Mr. Anderson to respond.

And Mr. Anderson had a plan. But he might need some backup. I made another call. Then I donned a dark blue polo shirt, khakis, sneakers, and a baseball cap. The dress code for Speedy Geek techs. (I'd staked them out on a few calls to get the uniform right.)

Velvet met me around the corner from the TFC. She'd brought Winter with her. I was a little disappointed since I'd wanted the chance to talk to Velvet again. I thought we'd gotten past the weirdness between us.

"Are you sure you want to do this?" Winter asked.

"Just be on the lookout for anyone dressed like me," I told them, annoyed. "Or anybody else suspicious." Cops. Black vans. Helicopters.

"Oh, he loves this secret-squirrel, con-man stuff," Velvet said, smiling. "Don't worry, we've got your back, Neo."

I wasn't sure how to take that, so I just pulled on my cap and acted like I was Tom Anderson come to set up the new system.

I managed to reverse tailgate someone coming out the door. He held it open for me without a second glance. The smells of fresh paint, new carpet, and plastic assaulted my gag reflex as I crossed the smooth tile floor. At the counter, I announced myself. "Tech support."

A girl with sleek black hair popped up from behind the counter. "Oh, thank goodness." She'd been trying to move a potted plant across the carpeted floor to the other side of the office area.

"Let me help you with that," I said, and Mr. Anderson leaped into action. She pointed to where she wanted it, and I dutifully dragged it into place. When I looked up, she was leaning across the counter, smiling at me. She was cute and couldn't be more than eighteen, nineteen tops. I smiled back.

"Anything else I can do for you . . . ?" I left the last word hanging there for her to fill in the blank.

And she did. "Sati. Sati Chandra."

"Tom Anderson." I wiped off my hands and stepped

closer to her. "Are you new here? With the company, I mean?" I leaned against the counter.

"Yes, I just started." She flicked her long black hair to one side. "Not many of the old staff wanted to come back," she whispered confidentially. "Mr. Anderson."

"Sucks what happened." I nodded sympathetically.

"Suck happens," she said with a sigh. She casually rolled her wrist over to reveal a small, perfect circle tattoo there.

I blinked a few times, thrown completely off my game. Then I just as casually tucked a piece of hair behind my right ear and revealed an identical tattoo on my neck. I had Mr. Yamada give me "the special" right after Velvet had hers done. Sati slipped me a Post-it note, which I quickly stuffed into my pocket.

The guy who'd let me in appeared again—with a ladder. He shook his head at the two of us practically joined at the hip already. He leaned the step ladder against the far lobby wall, his back to us. He was installing the security cameras.

"I hear you have a little computer problem," was the only thing I could think to say at that point.

"I can't get the darn thing on the network," she said, jabbing her thumb at the terminal behind her.

"Log in for me so I can see if there's something up with your user setup," I said, all business again.

She did so without hesitation and then moved aside for me to take the reins. My fingers flew over the keyboard, disabling any keystroke monitoring and other security countermeasures. "I'd kill for a coffee, if you have any," I told Sati with a woeful look on my face.

She touched my shoulder lightly. "Of course, Tom. I'll make us all a pot." She disappeared into the back.

The guy on the ladder chuckled, his back still to me.

I slipped a data cube out of my khakis and placed it in the reader. The terminal swallowed the blue pill and plugged itself into my own version of the Matrix. To the casual user, the terminal appeared to be on the TFC network, but I now had remote access to it from the MemeNet. Theoretically, the hack wasn't detectable. But I could deploy a "red pill" from my mobile or a terminal at work (anywhere really) to destroy the link.

I put the data cube back in my pocket and restored the terminal to the network.

Sati returned with paper cups filled with coffee, one for me, one for her, and one for the ladder dude.

"You're a genius, Neo," she said, taking one look at the screen. She kissed me on the cheek. "I mean, Mr. Anderson."

I took my coffee to go, but I peeked at the slip of paper in my pocket, just to make sure she'd given me her digits.

The purple square of paper said: Trinity303.

SOMETHING EPIC THIS WAY COMES

VELVET

Aiden didn't need backup. He came out of there with a cup of coffee, pale pink lipstick on his cheek, and a dazed look on his mug. Part of me was unexpectedly jealous. Part of me was relieved.

"Done?" Winter asked.

He nodded. "Keep walking," he said. "Ahead of me. Just in case anyone is watching. We'll catch the bus at the corner. You guys head to Mr. Yamada's, and I'll see you later."

"You take the bus. We'll walk," I said and picked up the pace. Right past the bus stop.

Winter hesitated and then followed me. Once we were nearly halfway to her grandfather's house, she stopped me. "Okay, I thought you two talked."

"We did."

"Then why did you insist I come with you?"

"Spike's a little touchy about me and Aiden being alone together."

"Uh huh," Winter said as she turned those damned X-ray eyes of hers on me.

It was true, but if I were completely honest, I was the one who was touchy about being alone with Aiden. There was still a spark of something there. But I'd made my choice. Spike was who I needed right now, and I kept telling myself that every time I saw Aiden.

I shrugged. "It's easy with Spike. He's been there for me. He gets me, good and bad." And I liked the way he made me feel.

Winter was silent for a moment. "I know. Lina gets me that way, too." She smiled. "And she still likes me."

"But do *you* like her?"

Without hesitation, Winter said, "Yeah. Lina can build anything out of plastic and metal. She's funny. And she can run like the wind. She can even do Sasuke-san's crazy obstacle course—faster than he can."

I put my arm around Winter, glad that one of us was so sure about her relationship. We walked that way for a few blocks, until I saw a cop car pull over up ahead.

A woman cop got out, wand in hand, and waited for us. We were only a block or so from Mr. Yamada's house.

"Be cool," Winter whispered.

We both steeled ourselves to walk casually up to

the police officer. We were probably both thinking the same, though. What if the replacement chip didn't pass the cop scan? We'd be royally screwed. I eyed the back fence of Mr. Yamada's place, but if Aiden (and the dogs) had taught me anything, bluffing was the better course of action.

"Be confident," I whispered back.

"Ladies," the cop said simply. "May I check your IDs?"

"Of course," I said, walking up to her. She looked very familiar. Her badge said Sergeant Sheila Martin.

Winter followed, and we dutifully submitted to the wanding. The scanner chimed pleasantly twice.

Winter and I both let out our breaths slowly as the cop drove away.

Then as we approached Mr. Yamada's "back" entrance, Winter swore. The Nomura signs had been plastered over with VOTE MIGNON posters and HAKITA ELEC-TRONICS stickers. And I could hear the strains of "Anything Girl" coming out of the boys' "soundproof" studio inside the fence.

"We need to do something epic for this election," I said more to myself than to Winter. "The concert." We'd already decided to do one, but this sealed the deal. It gave us a why and when. "On the eve of the election, we need a giant Vote . . ." I couldn't think of the name of Mignon's opponent, and even then, I wasn't so sure she was any better. And an anti-someone concert didn't sit right. People needed

THE BITTER RED PILL OF AWAKENING

AIDEN

I decided to go home instead of going to Mr. Yamada's. I ditched the bus at the next stop and had Jao pick me up. A rich boy move, Velvet would have called it. I didn't care. I thought maybe we could start over, even if just as friends, but she'd made it clear that she didn't want that. She'd chosen Spike. But that's only fair. Winter thinks they'd been dating since the end of the school year. Of course, Winter doesn't remember much about that time. Anyway. Velvet and Spike had way more in common than she and I did. Music. School. Funky clothes. Everything.

Being all grown-up about it didn't make me feel any better.

But then there was Trinity303, aka Sati Chandra, in my pocket on a purple Post-it. She'd sussed out who I was. I was not as smooth as I thought I was. And obviously, not the only fan of old movies.

The house was quiet. Dad was helping Mom move back to the States. She could run her family's bank from here now that I was back from boarding school in Bern. Aunt Spring and Uncle Brian offered to let me stay with them, but I'd been spending a lot of time at Mr. Yamada's, recording MemeCasts, building hotspots, and generally keeping busy. It was good to collapse in my own bed and order a pizza.

After a shower, I sat on the bed with my mobile, a pizza, and a power drink. The fuel of many an epic hackathon. I had homework, too, but that wasn't going to happen tonight.

From my trusty Nomura Freedom, I was able to pull up the main menu of TFC No. 23's terminal. I poked around and rattled on a few doors until I hit the central TFC customer data store. The front end was just regular info: visits, reward points, credit data, etc. A few more not-so-well-guarded doors revealed what I'd been looking for: the actual sessions.

I searched for Nora's mother's sessions. Zero results for Sidney Woolf James or just Sidney Woolf or Sidney James.

Then I tried Jonas Wallenberg. Nada again. When I tried just Wallenberg, I got a hit for Sonia Reyes Wallenberg. The session was from nearly twelve years ago.

The universe muttered, and I opened that door.

Sonia Reyes Wallenberg was Jonas's wife, and Micah's mother.

It was what everyone was looking for—that final piece in the Jonas puzzle.

But after reading the transcript, I didn't know exactly what to do with it. Should I tell Micah? That might be like giving him the red pill and pulling the plug on his cozy Matrix version of his dad. The truth was almost as bad as the terrorist meme that was going around. Maybe I should nuke the record. But did I have a right to do that? Of course, I didn't really have a right to do what I was doing now.

I called Nora. And Winter. And even Velvet.

They all thought we should tell Micah the truth.

Neo101 wondered what to do about the records—and Trinity303.

32.0

THE INTERVENTIONISTS

MICAH

Picking the low-hanging fruit, the guy called it.

I was bumming around the empty apartment in my sweatpants doing my Saturday chores, with a new Meme-Cast blaring. Aiden had a guest 'caster on, talking about how we used up way more than half of the oil in the world ages ago. We can't make more dinosaurs, the dude said, but we keep using more and more of their energy. And our "interventions" in countries like Venezuela, Algeria, and Syria were all about the black gold. No matter what anyone says. He'd been there. Saudi Arabia was the next "fruit" to get plucked. The so-called "Coalition coup" was just a front to give us an excuse. Terrorists had not taken over the country as the media would like you to believe. Ordinary people had risen up and thrown out the oil-rich sheiks, and those were the people who were cutting us off, Dozer23 explained in a disguised voice. And those were the people we were going over there to fight.

It was a freaking scary subject for a Halloween morning—and it fit my mood.

I flicked on the ceiling fan. It was finally cooling off outside. A bit. The open windows—tiny though they were—let in a fresh October breeze, so the ceiling fan wasn't just pushing hot air around. I sank my teeth into the last Pop-Tart when the doorbell rang.

It was Nora, Velvet, and Winter—and Aiden—all looking very serious. Of course, Aiden recorded his shows and then randomly posted them. Their faces reminded me of that 'cast where friends and family confront their loved ones to make them go to rehab—or TFC.

"It's too early for trick-or-treaters. Is this an intervention or something?"

They weren't laughing.

I let them in, turned off the 'cast, and grabbed a dirty T-shirt from the laundry basket by the door. One of my weekend chores was doing the laundry in the tiny laundry room on the first floor. All the machines were taken. Sometimes you had to wait until late at night to get a free washer and dryer—and then hope the power didn't go out.

"Well, make yourself at home, if you can." I motioned to the two barstools and the lawn furniture in the living room. I'd picked up a few more cheap plastic chairs from a dumpster on Ninth. I didn't tell them where the furnishings were from. "The floor is probably the most comfortable part." Mr. Mao was firmly planted on the chaise lounge again.

"We brought treats." Velvet lifted a bag from the doughnut shop down the street and headed toward the kitchen. Winter followed with a tray of Styrofoam cups.

I sat on the kitchen counter stirring my coffee while my friends made themselves "comfortable." Winter and Velvet snagged the barstools. Aiden leaned against the counter opposite me, and Nora stood by the sink.

"Aiden's got something to show you," Nora blurted out.

He glanced at Nora with a distinct oh-no-you-didn't-just-throw-me-under-the-bus look. Then he started talking. "Nora asked me to do a little digging—in the TFC customer database—about your dad, among other things."

Nora glared at him when he said the last part.

Aiden shifted uncomfortably and then put down the coffee he hadn't been drinking. He pulled out a folded sheet of paper from his back pocket.

"I found your Mom's only session. She's talking about your dad's—death." He held it out to me. "You can listen to the session if you want, but it might be easier to read it first."

I didn't move. Nora took the paper and placed it in my hands. "You should know the truth," she said.

My hands trembled as I unfolded the paper.

The apartment was silent while I read, except for the rhythmic turns of the ceiling fans. Some of the words wouldn't stay put on the page—especially toward the end.

Finally, I couldn't read anymore. I got the gist of it, and that made me clench the paper in my fist. I wanted to crush the words into nothingness.

Nora touched my arm and I flinched. I'd almost forgotten they were all there, trying not to look at me. "Sorry," I choked out.

"No, man, we're sorry," Aiden said. Velvet and Winter both said something equally as comforting and meaningless. I knew they all meant it, even Aiden.

"You okay?" Nora whispered.

I shook my head. How could I be okay?

"Dumb question," she said and took my hand.

"I just need some time," I mumbled.

Everyone nodded and hugged me on the way out, all telling me to call if I needed anything. Nora kissed me, but even that was no comfort.

I sank into a lawn chair and stared at the ceiling fan for a while. Mr. Mao crawled into my lap and purred quietly against my stomach. Oddly, that was the one thing that made me feel a little better.

Mom's story fit, but it wasn't what I'd expected. I smoothed out the paper I was still clutching in my hand and re-read the words.

The transcript was dated a few days after the date on Dad's tombstone.

Subject: Sonia Reyes Wallenberg

[Subject] I had to work that evening at Hamilton Memorial. Night shift in the ER. Somebody had to bring in some money. Jonas had quit his last job, and then Los Palamos Hospital let me go. We lost our house in LP, too. All I could get were sub shifts.

Jonas usually took care of Micah, our pequeño, when I worked nights. That night, Jonas wanted to take our toddler to this concert he had organized. It was in Thomas Park. I didn't like the idea, but we couldn't get a sitter. Everyone we knew was going to this event. Jonas swore it was safe. "Nothing but a concert in the park on a summer's evening," he said. And he'd worked so hard to make this thing happen. It was good to see him working at something again. I couldn't say no.

Jonas was a man who threw himself into everything. All or nothing. It was how he dealt. He threw himself into "activism" because of his experience with PTSD. The treatments he helped pioneer at TFC weren't working anymore.

[TFC Operative] Pioneered?

[Subject] Yes. The army had been his life for so long. He quit—medical discharge—because of his PTSD. Nothing really worked. None of the antidepressants or therapies the Veterans Administration gave him helped. Then he discovered clinical trials TFC was doing for a new drug:

Ameliorol. They recruited combat vets to test it on. It worked. And Jonas threw himself into working for the company, promoting the drug to other vets, helping build clinics. It was his life—until one day he walked away. The drug had stopped working, he said. The bad dreams, the mood swings, the paranoia, it all came back.

So he threw himself into working against the company.

[TFC Operative] This was that anti-TFC concert?

[Subject nodded.] Yes, I should never have let either of them go.

At work that evening, we got the call that ambulances were bringing in casualties from the concert. A riot had broken out when the police tried to break it up. People had been crushed, beaten, and worse.

I called Jonas. No answer. I called everyone I knew. Some didn't answer, either. Those that did hadn't seen Jonas and Micah since the concert started.

I panicked and jumped in my car. I flicked on the radio as I left the hospital parking lot, and the news said people had gotten killed and many more had been arrested. I drove like a maniac to get home.

When I got there, Jonas was sitting on the front stoop, covered in blood and weeping incoherently. Without Micah. I shook Jonas until I finally got out of him that he'd lost Micah in the crowd. He'd put him up on stage to protect him when the police attacked in riot gear. The surge of the crowd pulled him away from Micah. Jonas fought his way back, even through a few cops with nightsticks, but our boy was gone. Jonas had come home to see if someone had brought Micah there.

After he got that out, he was crazed, tearing around looking for the baby. But I lost it. I screamed at him for "losing the one good thing left in my life." That shut him up. I said so many other things I didn't really mean. I was trembling with rage and fear.

Jonas pulled himself together and went back out to search for Micah. I called some neighbors and fellow MLSG members to help him look.

[TFC Operative] MLSG?

[Subject] The Memory Loss Support Group. It was this support group Jonas had founded for other people involved in the drug trials. At least it began that way.

Anyway. Then Mrs. B came walking up the sidewalk with Micah slumped against her shoulder, sound asleep and perfectly fine. I was so relieved and thankful. And I immediately regretted all the nasty things I'd said to Jonas—though I was still mad, mostly at myself, for letting him take Micah in the first place. I knew Jonas's state of mind wasn't the best, but I'd been so angry and scared.

Jonas didn't come home that night. I called and called him. (The police even came looking for him, so I knew they didn't have him.) I combed the neighborhood while Mrs. B watched Micah. I sent other MLSG members to look for him.

Finally, someone found his body floating in the river

under the Thirteenth Street Bridge. A note tucked in his pocket said he couldn't forgive himself for endangering his son. It said some other stuff about not being able to cope or provide for his family.

[Subject sobs.]

So that was the great mystery of my dad. He didn't die in Detention or at the hands of the police. He'd killed himself. Because of me.

And I didn't know how I was supposed to feel. My brain knew it wasn't my fault, or really his, but I still felt guilty and angry and betrayed and sad, all at the same time. I didn't know where one feeling stopped and the other started. Or what to do about it.

I thought about skating down to the greenway, to Thomas Park and the bridge, places I'd been hundreds of times before I knew this.

But I couldn't.

Instead, I pushed all the lawn furniture into the kitchen and skated the bare living room until the lady downstairs started thumping on the ceiling. It didn't clear my head. I knew it wouldn't. I knew the only thing that would. Sort of.

I got out my sketch pad.

33.0

NOT ALL THE MONSTERS ARE IN THE MOVIES

NORA

I went back a few hours later. We'd planned to watch old monster movies for Halloween, but I knew Micah wouldn't be into that now. He was lying in the middle of his bare living room floor, surrounded by a sea of sketches.

He handed me his sketch pad as I sat down beside him. He had the next *Memento*, maybe even the next two, fully inked. He'd told his dad's story, from high school through the suicide. He'd ended with himself and Mr. Kowalcyk by his dad's grave.

"It needs words," Micah said, handing me the pen.

We spread out on the floor, our heads down, our arms lightly touching, as we finished *Memento*. Micah nodded with approval as I put in Mr. K's words at the end: "He wanted to fix more than tanks. . . . He wanted to run for Congress someday."

When I looked at the final sheets, that feeling was back again, that one of having produced something real and good.

Micah scanned and uploaded the comics—a two-parter —to the MemeNet. Then he looked at me. "Well, that's my dad problem figured out. How about yours?"

I laughed.

I'd been thinking about that a lot.

"I think I need to tell the truth, too." I pulled my sleeve up, revealing the greening bruises on my wrist. It still throbbed. I could hear Micah's sharp intake of air. I hadn't planned on showing him this. I just came to be here for him—and thought I'd deal with me later. I was the queen of not dealing lately. (*Wow, I'm beginning to sound like Velvet.*) After I left earlier, I didn't go home. The others went wherever, but I bussed it to the mall, hoping to lose myself in window-shopping. It didn't help. All I could think about was how Micah's mom unburdened herself at TFC to deal with his dad. My mom had done the same exact thing, only for different reasons. And I realized, as I stared at a pair of pink gel mary janes in the Shoe City window, that I hadn't truly believed Mom about the abuse until Dad actually hurt me. How shallow is that? Maybe that's why I keep not telling her. Shame.

"Your dad did this?" Micah asked wide-eyed.

I nodded.

He leaped to his feet. "I will punch his lights out."

"No, you won't," I said, rising to my feet. "I need to tell my mom." And probably testify against my dad in court, I realized with a hard swallow.

"Okay, let's go now." Micah headed toward the door, still full of that need to do something, anything. I loved him all the more for it.

I nodded. "But first put on a shirt. And shoes."

GOING TO SEE THE ORACLE

VELVET

"Take a couple of the dogs with you," Mom yelled after us. "At least take that one," she said with an odd smile as she pointed to the big black dog standing by the door.

I grabbed one of the leashes from the rack and clipped it on her collar. Winter and Lina (Lina mostly) picked out the spastic border collie, Lucky, to walk. Dad just grabbed the cane Mom thrust at him. His limp had gotten much better, but it came back if he walked a long distance—like down to Thomas Park. He pecked Mom on the cheek, and we were off again.

The crisp morning air felt wonderful. The leaves were bright oranges and deep reds, and the sky was blue. Bridget plodded along beside me as we crunched through the leaves. A few vacant houses had gotten TPed last night. But all in all, the day was not too shabby. Except everyone else was in their own little world. Winter and Lina walked ahead arm-in-arm, Lucky pulling them happily along. And Dad was quiet.

I left him to his thoughts as we walked toward Thirteenth Street.

The concert was coming together. The boys had discovered they really did know the songs I'd written for the last (and only) concert. Today they were practicing the new material. Richie had kidded that we really didn't need anything new, since nobody remembered the old stuff anyway. But two other bands—the Minor Birds and Agent Smith—had contacted us about playing, too. So the Wannabes had to be sharp. As soon as I put it out on the MemeNet that we were planning this gig, we got so many other people—complete strangers—offering to help.

The problem was we didn't have a venue completely nailed down. I made out like we did but were keeping it secret until the last minute for security reasons. That way the other bands wouldn't bail. We couldn't use the Twinkie Factory again because it was going condo. A TFC condo. Besides, having it at some abandoned building again just didn't seem like the way to go.

Then we heard Mr. Wallenberg's story—and the last *Memento* told it to the world—and the place was obvious: Thomas Park. It was the site where he'd organized his concert against TFC all those years ago. Our concert was going to be a tribute to him, so it was a natural fit.

It's probably why Dad hadn't said a word on our walk down here. As we passed under the bridge, past the U-cycle racks, Dad stopped to pull something out of his pocket. A small flag. He leaned on his cane as he knelt and planted the flag in a spot by the water. He stayed there for a few moments and then hauled himself up and brushed off his jeans. "Okay, V, let's go see this Oracle of yours," he said with renewed energy.

Oracle was the MemeNet name of the unofficial mayor of Thomas Park. That's what other park vendors, gardeners, and residents called her. I contacted the Oracle about having the concert here. She was game as long as we didn't plan on running anybody out. "Of course not; we could use their help," had been my response. I'd never envisioned *not* having the park people at the concert. This was one of Mom's favorite places to barter, and she even worked the food bank "booth" down here sometimes.

"Who are we looking for, Velvet?" Winter asked.

"A bread vendor along the bike path," I told her.

Dad took it in as we walked down the greenway, passing raised gardens and stalls filled with apples, cabbages, chili peppers, and pumpkins. The fruit sellers were from farms outside of Hamilton. There were also people selling crafty stuff: candles, pottery, and jewelry. Winter and Lina got distracted by a gal selling electronic scrap. My eye wandered toward a tent selling old clothes. The hand-painted sign said HUXLEY'S CLOTHES SWAP.

"When did all this happen?" Dad asked.

I shrugged but made a mental note of the vintage booth. "Maybe a year or two ago. Nothing as big as this until lately."

The scent of coffee and sausage—and bread—wafted toward me. A hot dog vendor parked his cart off the greenway, on the river side, just ahead. On the other side, I saw a sign hanging from a table laden with bread, cookies, and muffins. The sign said MT. ZION BAKERY. Bridget pulled at the lead in that direction.

As we neared it, a tall black woman with short gray hair (and penetrating gray eyes) peered at us and then broke into a smile.

"Oracle?" I asked.

Instead of greeting me, the woman bent to hug the black dog who was now licking her face. She grabbed something from a paper bag and snapped her fingers. Bridget dutifully lay down, and the Oracle tossed the happy dog a bone-shaped biscuit.

"Mrs. Brooks," Dad said.

"As in Micah's Mrs. Brooks from Black Dog Village?" I asked. Understanding broke through my brain. The black dog of Black Dog Village begged for another treat. Sneaky Mom knew who I was meeting all along. But how did Dad know her?

"Little Travis Kowalcyk," Mrs. Brooks said with a smile. "Your daughter is a better poet than you ever were." She turned to me. "Your dad skated by senior English when he had so much potential. They didn't call him Dozer because he could operate heavy machinery."

"The Oracle, huh?" Winter asked as she walked up. Lina was cleaning up after Lucky.

"I always liked that old movie," Mrs. Brooks said. "And I'm always glad to see Micah's friends. Should we get down to business?" she asked, turning back to me.

We retreated into the tent just behind the main table while a slender white lady took over the selling. Mrs. B served up apple cider and fresh blueberry muffins while we discussed the concert setup. I pointed out where the stage and lighting ought to go. Dad and Winter had volunteered to handle the power for the lighting and sound equipment. Dad could hook up generators and Winter a few solar panels to run the show. They downed their ciders and went out to measure everything. Lina and Big Steven, who had shown up just as they were leaving the tent, followed to help. Mrs. B and I worked out what else needed to be done, from getting grass mowed to security and contingency plans. When Dad got back, everything was set.

"You should be proud of this one, Travis," Mrs. Brooks said as we were leaving. "She gets things done." That seemed like her highest praise.

"I am," Dad said as he put his arm around me. Then he went quiet again.

As we walked back out of the park, past the U-cycle racks and under the bridge, Dad finally said what was on his mind. "I hope this concert doesn't turn out like the one Jonas organized."

I hoped not either. *Or like the last one I organized.*

Someone once said the definition of crazy was doing the same thing over and over again and expecting different results. Maybe sometimes you've got to keep knocking on the door until the people on the other side are ready to crack it open a hair—or at least are annoyed enough to get up off the couch. *Book of Velvet.* Chapter 39, Verse 7.

The spot where Dad had stuck his memorial offering now sprouted a few more tiny flags and a bouquet of flowers.

FACING THE MEMELASH

MICAH

Mr. Mao lay curled up in a warm, purring, twelve-pound ball on my chest as I stared at the ceiling of my bedroom.

"*Mijo*, you can't miss another day, excused or not," Mom called up from the kitchen.

She was right. I was going to flunk out if I didn't go back to school. I couldn't afford to do that, if I ever hoped to get into art college—even the crappy one in Hamilton. We didn't have the money or points to transfer schools. Plus, when he heard what happened, Mr. Jeffries hired me part-time at the food bank, so I needed to be close by. Mom had looked into the online and night school options, but they felt like a cop-out to me.

Extricating myself from the fur bowling ball that was my cat, I dragged myself to my feet.

I couldn't go out that way. Quitting like a punk loser. I was tired of running and being afraid. And I actually missed school. Crazy, I know. I missed getting elbowed in the hall, the stupid lectures on cellular mitosis, the crappy mystery-meat lunches, and, most of all, hanging out at the freaks table with my friends.

So I pulled on my jeans and the cleanest T-shirt I could find, packed my messenger bag, and grabbed my skateboard. As I headed down the ladder from my loft-like area, Mr. Mao resumed his position in the person-shaped hollow I'd left in the bed. I envied him.

Mom was still in her pink robe—the one I'd gotten her for Christmas last year—sitting at the kitchen counter, sipping weak black coffee as she scanned the job ads on her mobile. She smiled tiredly at me and pushed a bowl of oatmeal in my direction. She looked as if she'd worked a triple shift and then slept in a car, badly.

"*Llego el Pacheo*," Mom said with a sigh as she held up her mobile. *Winter is coming.*

Literally she'd said, "Pacheo was coming." It was an old Venezuelan saying. I'd heard it come out of her mouth so many times when the first flake fell that I'd repeated it once in Spanish I conversation practice. The Anglo teacher just stared at me. "Who is Pacheo?" he asked as the class sniggered. Then I had to explain that in Caracas—where Mom was born—Pacheo was this farmer dude who came down from the mountains whenever it started to get cold. The people of Caracas would see him entering the city gates and know winter was on its way.

However, during the war, the saying took on a new meaning. "Winter (or Pacheo) is coming" became code for American troops—or trouble in general—coming into the city.

So Mom wasn't necessarily talking about a chill in the air.

I grabbed the last two Pop-Tarts—my least favorite flavor, brown sugar cinnamon—out of the box in the bare cabinet. I pushed the oatmeal in front of her. "What if I got another part-time job?" I asked.

"Don't you dare, Micah Jonas Wallenberg." Mom's eyes flashed at me and then softened. "You need to go back to school. Let me worry about the money."

I did. Need to go back, that is.

"It'll be okay, *mijo*," she said. "Just try to stay out of trouble."

Nodding, I kissed her on the top of the head and left.

Outside, I stuffed the Pop-Tarts into my bag and pushed off toward Homeland High No. 17. Whatever people said or did, I would keep my trap shut. For her.

The rent-a-cop at the door gave me an extra thorough pat down before he let me even walk through the scanner. If this had been an airport, I'd probably have gotten a full cavity search.

As I walked down the hall, I could feel every eye in the school on me. People parted before me like I had the plague. I just looked straight ahead until I got to my locker. I stuck my thumb in the scanner, right into some tacky goop. Glue, I hoped. The green light came on, but when I pulled the handle, the door wouldn't budge. Definitely glue. The surface of the locker had been tagged and scrubbed and retagged with various grafitti about being a terrorist or traitor. But I could also see the outlines of other well-scrubbed phrases. Jonas lives. Memento. And there were a few circles, too.

The silence around me was almost deafening. I turned to face the stares. Chuck Martin, one of the football jocks who'd beat me up last year, stood there with his crew of letter-jacketed apes right behind him. I met his eye and braced myself.

"Flatten the bastard," one of Martin's friends urged.

Chuck Martin stepped closer, but I didn't back down. There really wasn't anywhere I could go, anyway. Staring into my eyes, he tugged his letter jacket sleeves up a bit, and I steeled myself for the pummeling. Instead, Chuck Martin, captain of the football team, rolled his left wrist over just enough to reveal a perfect circle tattoo.

He winked. "Skaterboy is not worth the trouble," he said as he backed away. "And anyone who touches him will answer to me." Martin led his grumbling crew down the hall.

A few other kids nodded, and one or two others flashed tattoos at me as they passed by.

Maybe winter wouldn't suck too bad this year after all.

HUMMINGBIRD'S-EYE VIEW

WINTER

I zipped up my hoodie—the one Lina had made—and perched myself on the low-pitched gable of the former Mt. Zion AME Church to drink my coffee. The painted brick building wasn't very tall, but I still had a nice view of Thomas Park across the river. The trees had turned radiant oranges and golds and reds. People were walking and biking the greenway, buying or bartering at the stalls, and playing catch with their kids (or dogs). I had the urge just to sit here, sip coffee, and watch.

This was something I never, ever did. Just sit. I always had to be doing something, anything. A project. But this morning, I felt like I could breathe. And no hummingbird flitted around in my brain.

The distant sounds of hammering punctuated the quiet

of an otherwise perfect Saturday morning. In the grassy area of the park, near the woods, volunteers were completing the stage for Velvet's concert. Mrs. B—aka the Oracle—had coordinated nearly all the labor, from the mowing to the Porta Potties. And she was spearheading this project, too.

The ladder creaked as Lina climbed up. "Dude, I thought you'd be finished by now," she said as she pulled herself up next to me. Behind me lay the thin-film solar panels we were supposed to be installing.

"Just waiting for you."

We crawled over to the where I'd laid out the panels and tools. Lina might be part of the reason I feel calmer now, but just part. Except for school, which was a complete bore despite its so-called higher academic standards, everything in my life was good. Whole. For once I had no big gaping holes that needed filling. Mom and Dad were back in my life. They were talking to my grandfather. My friends were all in one piece. I had my art—and these projects. And I had Lina.

I shook off the faintest flutter of hummingbird wings in my head.

Lina cleared her throat, and I handed her a socket wrench.

"Dad has this crazy idea we'll have enough kids for team sports." Lina chattered on about her parents' plan for the school. That's why we were powering up this abandoned church. The Walshes—Lina's parents—and

Mrs. Brooks had been teaching several off-grid kids in the park ever since the Community School was shut down. Lina's parents had taught there. Now they had a brainwave to fix up this place and hold classes here. The weather would soon get too cold to teach in a tent or even a storage locker.

I nodded whenever Lina paused for air. Sometimes it was nice just to listen. After the panels were secure, I dropped the power line down through the squat little steeple in the middle of the roof. As I sipped my now-lukewarm coffee, nodding appropriately at one of Lina's comments, I noticed a dark figure on a bike heading across the bridge from the park.

The hummingbirds fluttered to life in my brain.

"We're going to have company," I said, pointing out the figure to Lina. I tossed my coffee over the side.

We both scrambled down the ladder. "Better warn your folks and Mrs. Brooks," I told her, though I didn't need to. As soon as her feet hit the ground, she was already dashing around to the back of the building. The Walshes were painting and cleaning the old Sunday school rooms.

I plopped myself down on the front stoop of the church next to the crooked wooden sign that said Mt. Zion African Methodist Episcopal Church, founded 1946. I watched the cop push his bike along the uneven path from the river. He remounted once he reached the parking lot of the storage facility and then glided across it to the church.

Lina emerged from the church and sat down next to

me on the brick steps. She took my tattooed hand in hers that was similarly tattooed—one perfect circle covering another. She leaned over and kissed me—and then unzipped my hoodie.

"Wish I'd worn mine," she said.

"Are you cold? Want it?" I started to shrug mine off to give it to her.

She stopped me. "No, you keep it for now." Then she winked.

The girl was up to something.

The bike cop cleared his throat, and we realized he was standing in front of us in his bike shorts, watching us. "What are you young ladies doing here?" He pointedly glanced up to the roof. He'd obviously seen us up there.

"We're just helping fix up the church," I said. Velvet always says the best lies start with the truth.

"School project," Lina added.

The cop nodded. He looked dubious, though. "I have to check your IDs anyway." He unclipped the wand from his utility belt.

Taking a deep breath, I stood up first. My ID chip had passed cop muster when Velvet and I were stopped. But I wasn't sure about Lina's. She'd never gotten one in the first place, and she was one of the first we tried Aiden's hack with. He still wasn't sure it would hold, even after a few weeks of circulation.

The cop waved the scanner behind my ear. The wand chimed. He nodded, satisfied, and motioned for Lina to stand. She did, but I could tell she was nervous. I took her hand when it started to shake a tiny bit. The cop passed the wand behind her ear.

No chime. But no *bzzt* as the wrong type of sound, either.

Her grip tightened.

The cop looked puzzled. He wanded her again. Same thing.

"Is there a problem, officer?" I heard myself saying.

"Ms. Walsh here obviously has the proper ID, but something isn't syncing up right with headquarters." He shook the scanner. "I might have to take you in to check."

Crap. It was Aiden's worst fear—and mine. I thought furiously as the cop tinkered with the settings. The hummingbirds descended, trying to fill up my brain. I brushed them away.

Lina leaned over and zipped up my hoodie. "You look chilly, dear," she said when the cop noticed.

The hoodie. Of course. She is brilliant.

"Your scanner must be on the fritz," I said to the cop. "Try me again."

He did, and this time there was no pleasant chime.

Lina had modified the fabruino microcontrollers she'd sewn into the hoodie to jam radio signals like the one the scanner used.

The cop shook the scanner again and then reholstered it.

We held our breaths as he looked us over. His eyes

stopped on our hands. I suddenly felt a fear I'd never even considered. We were two girls holding hands, not like friends, in front of a cop. That wasn't illegal, of course. (Not like having fake IDs in our skulls.) But what if he was one of those antiquated bigots that thought the Marriage Equality Act never should've been passed? Would he give us a hard time just because he could?

Lina uncurled her fingers from mine.

The cop looked up at us with an odd little smile. He peeled off his fingerless bike gloves and stuck them in his belt. "You have a nice day, ladies." Then he extended his right hand to me. On his palm was a perfect circle.

After Officer Anthony James rode away, Lina and I sank onto the stoop of the future home of the Mt. Zion Community School in giddy relief.

"You are a fricking genius," I told her.

"And you were so cool, but we were damned lucky. Not every cop is going to be one of us."

I knew it. The thought of almost losing Lina—and the thought of all those people in the park or at the concert—made the hummingbird wings beat wildly in my head. "How many of these hoodies can you make by next week?"

"Not nearly enough," she said glumly. "But maybe some buttons? Maybe the folks on the MemeNet can do the same."

And maybe that would give my mother and Aiden time to come up with something else.

The sound of hummingbird wings dulled to a soft flutter.

MemeCast 2.19—

E-DAY MINUS ONE

Okay, citizens. Neo here. I'm going to keep this short and sweet because I've got a coffee date with a certain Trinity303 (IRL) in a few.

Tomorrow is the big day: Election Day. I know there's no one you really want to vote for. The choice is Mignon and some other suit backed by some other corporation. (Yes, Wallace did finally get a backer, but too little, too late.) But I was thinking. Actually, I had this message from Tank23 to remind folks about the write-in spot on the ballot. I'm not sure how it works, but what if you could send the winners a message? That would be the ultimate hack, right? The "None of the above" choice.

So go vote and then come by Thomas Park tomorrow evening for a post-election concert. And don't forget to read the latest Memento; man, it's a heartbreaker.

In the news, MiamiHeatFan33 says the gas stations are closed in his city. Wolkpack19 reports that they're seeing more and more empty shelves at the Food Lion down in Charlotte. Dozer23 tells me he's been called back, this time to Qatar, which he points out is on the Saudi border. He's heard there might be another "intervention" coming around Christmas. And he doesn't know how to tell his family.

Oh, and the MemeNet count? Off the charts.

And now to kick off this block of music, "Starters" by Agent Smith.

THE FORFEITURE OF ETHAN JAMES

NORA

"You don't have to do this." Mom took my hand as we sat in an empty judge's chamber of the Hamilton Domestic Relations District Court. We were waiting for Dad and his lawyer to show up. "I can do all the talking," Mom said with a squeeze of my hand.

I did need to do this, though. I looked at the greening bruises on my wrist. Micah had gone with me to tell Mom about Dad. She'd gasped, sobbed, and raged against him—and herself. I was almost sorry I'd told her. Almost. Then I told her—with Micah prompting me—that Dad planned to move us to Germany soon. That set a whirlwind in motion. Mom did her lawyer thing, talked to all the right services, pulled in a few favors, and we soon had this date in family court to reconsider who I was going to live with.

But that meant I needed to confront Dad. I hadn't seen him since Mom got a temporary injunction, or whatever, so I didn't have to go back to Los Palamos.

My charm bracelet dangled from the same wrist he'd nearly broken. Though I didn't remember it, he'd given me the bracelet and the first charm, a little purse, after my first trip to TFC. That's when I'd learned that he hit Mom. He'd given me the book charm after I got out of the Big D. He'd given me the last charm after he'd grabbed my arm. I had to say enough before I had a full bracelet of charms. I'd worn the bracelet today to remind myself of that. Each glossy bit of silver was a memento of the kind of guy Dad really was.

"No, I need to do it," I finally said to Mom.

The door in front opened to admit the judge, a silver-haired woman, and a uniformed sheriff's deputy. He stood by the door while she settled into her seat behind the desk.

"Judge Munoz," Mom said by way of greeting.

"Counselor," the judge acknowledged Mom without glancing up from the papers on her tablet screen. She peered over her tortoise-shell glasses at the empty desk beside us. In a way, I hoped Dad wouldn't show. But I wanted it to be over, too.

"What if he doesn't come?" I whispered to Mom.

"I'll find Mr. James in contempt," the judge answered for her.

The door behind us opened, and I heard footsteps

and the sounds of expensive suits rustling. I didn't look until Dad and his Armani-suited lawyer sat down at the table beside us. The judge glared at them, but it rolled off them as if their suits were made of Kevlar.

Judge Munoz banged her gavel and then read some words about the case. She talked, then Mom did, and the other lawyer answered. The words didn't sink into my skull; I was too busy telling myself to breathe slowly as I watched Dad. He wouldn't even look at me. He stared straight ahead.

"Nora?" Mom said gently—and I realized the judge had asked me something. "Can you tell the judge what happened?"

I glanced over at Dad again, who still wouldn't look in my direction. I nodded. "Do I need to go up there or stand?"

"No, honey," the judge said. "You tell me from there."

I took a deep breath and started talking about the party. I told her about overhearing Dad say we were moving to Hamburg, about interrupting them and bumping Ms. Foster-Caine. "Then, in the kitchen, he grabbed my arm hard and twisted it hard."

"Objection, your honor. My client asserts this was an accident—" Dad's lawyer began to say.

The judge raised her hand and he fell silent. "You'll have your chance to speak, Mr. Merovich." The judge motioned me forward.

She examined my wrist and the pictures Mom had the ER doctor take of it.

"Miss James, are you afraid of your father?" the judge asked gently.

I could feel Dad finally looking at me. All I could manage was a nod.

Then Dad whispered something to his lawyer and walked out of the judge's chambers. The slick lawyer in his Armani suit muttered that his client was no longer contesting custody of the minor. The judge said it didn't matter. Mom got sole custody, and Dad got charged with contempt. And the judge said she'd have him investigated further on the abuse charges. In the meantime, he'd only have supervised visitation at the discretion of my mother.

We'd won, but the victory somehow felt hollow as we watched Mr. Merovich leave the room.

38.0

EARLY DISMISSAL

MICAH

The numbers on the clock seemed stuck at 1:37 p.m. while my biology teacher was blah blah blahing about bacteria, Alexander Fleming, and antibiotics. Time probably wouldn't seem to crawl half as much if we weren't getting out early because it was Election Day. We still had a lot to do to get ready for the concert.

I half- (or maybe quarter-) listened while I doodled. Fleming was this biologist dude who discovered penicillin because he let his lunch mold.

"He accidently revolutionized modern medicine," Ms. Graham pronounced, chuckling to herself. She was always doing that, and none of us ever got the joke.

Richie was beginning to nod off in front of me. Ms. G cleared her throat, which snapped him to attention.

Chuck Martin, who was sitting a few desks behind me, stifled a laugh.

"Tomorrow we're going to identify bacterial shapes and cell structures under the microscope. So I want you to watch this short video on how to use one." Ms. Graham flicked on the screen and dimmed the lights.

I kept doodling. It was more than a doodle, actually. It was something I'd been kicking around in my head for a while, and it was coming out way more stylized—more Dr. Seuss or Tim Burton—than the stuff I usually drew.

A line of people (or people-shaped objects) were being carried along a conveyor belt into this factory. In the next frame, a machine arm with spindly fingers popped open a person's skull and plugged in a chip. Then the person (product?) slid through the assembly line, getting his brained scrubbed in one frame, then getting something added in the next. Finally, the products rolled off the assembly line, some carrying shopping bags and some carrying rifles. Each group went their separate way but still received signals from the factory.

I hadn't named the factory yet, just in case, but the sign out front would have three letters.

"You should post that on the MemeNet, Skaterboy," Chuck Martin whispered. I hadn't noticed him slipping into the seat behind me. "Seriously."

"Mr. Martin," Ms. Graham intoned flatly. "Back to your seat and stop picking on Mr. Wallenberg, who should put away his sketch pad before I confiscate it."

I stuffed it into my bag as Chuck slinked back to his seat.

Ten interminable minutes later, the final bell rang.

Chuck Martin came up behind Richie and me as we made our exit. Chuck Martin, my archnemesis since, oh, kindergarten. Chuck Martin whose parents were both cops, and who seemed destined for the same thing. That Chuck Martin tucked a sticker into my hand and whispered, "Be careful at the park tonight. Half the police force will be there."

The sticker said: VOTE JONAS.

THE SHIT HITS THE FAN (AND DAD HITS THE ROAD)

NORA

After court, Mom and I had lunch and then took the bus to pick up my things in Los Palamos. Mr. Merovich assured Mom that Dad wouldn't be there. Something about a business trip. I wondered if he was already on his way to Germany. A Patriot Party ad scrolled across the seat screen. *Vote Mignon. Keep America Strong.* Then the news flashed a report on Coalition bombings in the Middle East. *Striking at the heart of the Coalition*, they quoted Mignon as saying, *will keep us safe.*

The bus stopped at the LP gates, and security in flak jackets boarded the bus to wand each of us and search our bags. The other people on the bus, mostly wearing uniforms of some sort, didn't seem surprised.

Soon we were standing outside the elevator of the Galleria Towers with Dad's lawyer. Neither he nor Mom said anything. He pressed the P button for penthouse and silently rode with us up the twenty-seven floors.

Mom gasped as she stepped off the elevator—and not because of the swankiness of the décor. The place looked like it had been ransacked. We both looked at the lawyer, but he suddenly became interested in the shine of his shoes and some call neither of us heard. I got it.

Dad had smashed everything breakable (and some things not so breakable) in the living area, kitchen, and in my room. My screen was in bits on the floor. My drawers had been emptied and smashed. My jewelry case was across the room. The air smelled like Eau de Lile, and a cracked bottle puddled on my bathroom floor. The contents of my bookshelf splayed out across the floor. One book lay in the center of my bed. Unopened.

"I should've come by myself," Mom said. "But I never imagined . . . Do want to salvage your clothes and jewelry?"

I was staring at the book on my bed. It was my history book from last term. The one with the MemeNet hotspot in it.

Mom grabbed a suitcase from the closet and started packing. I opened the book.

It was empty, and a page had been torn out. I frantically searched through the debris on the floor and even under the bed. Then I raced back out into the living room and into his den—empty. His room—empty.

Dad—the head of TFC's security goons—knew about the MemeNet. But he'd left. It didn't make sense. I confronted the lawyer.

"Where did he go?"

"I've already notified the court. Mr. James left the country this morning on business."

"Germany."

"That I can't say."

"Nora," Mom called from the kitchen. I found her reading a note beside an unbroken vase of slightly wilted flowers. She handed it to me. *Princess, I am so sorry and ashamed for how I acted. I never meant to hurt you. You are better off with your mother.*

"Mom, we need to go." As hurt as I was, all I could think about was that empty book. He'd torn out the page that said "Your father beats your mother," but he'd also taken the router. Did he know about the new *Memento*s? The MemeCast? The concert? "The special"? There were going to be a lot of people in Thomas Park tonight with illegal chips.

When we got down to the bus stop, I slipped my Nomura Freedom out of my pocket. No connection. And my hotspot was hardly the only one in LP. I pulled out my real phone and texted Aiden: MN down in LP.

Mom whispered over my shoulder, "Let's take a cab." The streetlights started to come on, and I noticed that it was beginning to get dark. And Mom had rescued a rolling suitcase of my stuff.

Aiden texted back an expletive—and that his driver, Jao, was on his way.

wearing gas masks outside TFC No. 23. And apparently so could many of the concertgoers. One lady—a perfectly respectable-looking teacher or lawyer type—did the universal I'm-watching-you thing at the cops in the car. The woman cop behind the wheel looked away.

The temporary lights Dad and his volunteers set up started to come on as the sun dipped behind the TFC tower downtown. The lights of the cityscape twinkled as it got darker. The weather was beautiful, still warm for November, and cicadas thrummed in the background. A perfect evening for a concert.

The Wannabes were going on first. Then Minor Birds and Agent Smith. The boys played the first strains of "Anything Girl"—one of my songs—and the crowd erupted with applause. For my song. Winter punched me in the arm. She and Lina were monitoring the MemeNet as the concert was going out over the network. Aiden was Meme-Casting from somewhere in the park. And Micah was handing out a new *Memento* he'd run off this afternoon.

Nothing beat this rush. I'd felt this way at the first rave, and I was still afraid this one was going to go the same way. On the other hand, I also felt like everything was going to be alright. Maybe that was just the applause going to my head, though. I kept one eye on the cops.

The boys played a few more songs as it got darker and more people streamed in. Mr. Yamada reported that everyone was behaving wonderfully—including the bike cops. Dad called to say the generators running the lights were doing fine as were Winter's solar-charged batteries running the sound equipment. We even had a few of them to spare, Lina informed me.

The Wannabes started in on "Spark," the last song of the set. I looked back toward the city—only to see darkness. Then Aiden panted up behind me.

"Nora just texted me. The MemeNet is out in Los Palamos. Green Zone knows about it."

"Is she okay?" Micah asked anxiously.

"I sent Jao to pick up her and her mom," Aiden reassured him. "They'll meet us at the rendezvous point."

Oh crap. I glanced toward the cop cars. The woman cop was opening her door.

"Is it still working here in the city?" I asked.

Aiden glanced at his mobile, though he probably already knew the answer. "Yep. Still going strong. Other cities checking in up and down the East Coast, too."

"Go to Defcon 2," I said. Lina, Winter, and Big Steven scrambled. I heard Winter warning her grandfather.

"I'll tell the guys," Micah added over his shoulder. "And get them to Mt. Zion before . . ." His last words were lost in the crowd.

But that was our plan. If the shit really hit the fan, we'd meet at the storage facility parking lot, where those with cars had parked them. The Oracle had her people from the homeless village guarding the old bridge that led to Mt. Zion.

Aiden stood by my side as the cops approached. The

Peterson kid picked up his bat, but I motioned for him to put it down. "Remember, no provoking the cops." He nodded, but he was a little too quick on the bat. "Go warn your people at the bridge," I told him, and he slipped through the crowd on his bike.

Winter slid a portable mike into my hand.

The woman cop and several others approached the park entrance. By the time she got there, a wall of people stood behind me. The boys were winding down their last number, and the Minor Birds were getting ready to go on. I could hear sirens approaching and see the outline of black vans crossing the Thirteenth Street Bridge.

"You're going to have to shut down the concert," the woman cop said. I recognized her. She was the same cop who'd wanded us a few days ago. And now I was sure. She was the same one I'd seen outside TFC No. 23. She'd thrown her gas mask down in disgust and told me to disappear.

"We have a permit," I said.

"I know," she said wearily. "That shit doesn't seem to matter anymore. And you know what's coming."

People behind me were getting angry, and her line of cops was tensing up, hands on nightsticks and worse. I could feel my hand starting to shake—and my feet didn't want to move forward. This was too much like my nightmares. Aiden squeezed my hand lightly. I couldn't let this situation turn out like the one in front of TFC No. 23.

White-knuckling the mike, I took a deep breath and

stepped out to meet the cop. She met me halfway. Yep, her badge said Sergeant Sheila Martin.

"Look, Sergeant Martin. Sheila. I saw you after the TFC bombing. You were angry and disgusted. And you know who did that—not the protestors—but *them*." I motioned to the vans pulling up behind the cop cars. "And I know you're sick of it."

Sergeant Martin shifted uncomfortably, and the rest of the cops glanced nervously around. I couldn't tell if I was getting through to her or them, or if they'd just noticed that my voice was going out all over Thomas Park (and the MemeNet).

I pressed on. "Isn't it time to say *enough*?"

All of a sudden I heard Micah's voice in the background, saying something to the crowd. Then I heard the boys and the Minor Birds start chanting off-mike—and the crowd picked it up. It took me a few seconds to figure out what they were saying. They were echoing me. "Enough."

Sheila Martin stood there looking at me—and the crowd—for another several long, long seconds. Green Zone security was closing the ranks behind her. One of my people called out a name. "Frank Reeves. You are my neighbor." The cop third from the end looked down.

The crowd intoned, "Enough."

Someone else said, "Sarah Parker. You're my sister-in-law." Another name was spoken, and then another—until practically the whole thin blue line had been called out.

One last voice rang out, "Sheila Martin, you are my

mother." A tall meat-headed guy in a Homeland High letter jacket stepped up next to me. Damn, if it wasn't Chuck Martin.

Sergeant Martin held up her hand, and the people behind me hushed. A soft, low chant still reverberated in the crowd. She glanced at the cops behind her, most of them nodding to her.

Then she turned and said one word to the Kevlar-encrusted guy with the tear gas-launcher, leading the pack of black van goons from Green Zone. Sergeant Sheila Martin said: "Enough."

I handed her the mike, and she said it again. And this time thousands of people behind me said it again, too. Loud and clear.

I imagined the listeners joining in up and down the MemeNet.

It was a start.

THE BEGINNING OF THE START

MICAH

The blackout lasted well into the morning. Everything was still off—except the MemeNet. (It had gone down in a few compounds but had quickly come back online.) I scanned it for news while Mom scrounged up breakfast.

She sniffed the milk and poured it down the sink. She settled on peanut butter sandwiches and warm juice boxes. We were out of Pop-Tarts so I scarfed down a PB&J and a bowl of dry Tastee Wheat on top of that.

The cops turning on the black van guys last night was all over the 'net—as was the concert and what Velvet said. I was damn proud of her. I don't know if I could have stood up to that cop like she did. But sometimes I guess you've got do what you've got to do. *Book of Velvet*. Or Micah.

I'd actually surprised myself with what I did. I'd pushed my way through the crowd and got to the stage just as the guys finished their set. Mr. Kowalcyk helped pull me up, and the weirdest thing happened. I was hit by a wave of déjà vu. I'd been pushed up onto this stage before. And for a second, I had this clear vision of my dad standing where I was standing as I took the mike. I saw him talking to a crowd and then getting hustled offstage and through the crowd to a waiting car—while a woman held me. I shook off the vision and turned to *my* crowd. Words came out of my mouth. I'm not sure what I said. Something about the cops and Green Zone being here, but we shouldn't run. We should stand our ground. We should say—

Velvet's voice came over the PA then, and she said the word I'd been searching for: "Enough." Then we were all chanting it.

After the cops left, the Minor Birds played like they were on fire. Midway through the set, Nora and her mom came walking up the greenway. Aiden's guy had dropped them off at Mt. Zion and then walked them over. Nora, Mrs. James, and I joined Velvet and the gang to enjoy the rest of the concert. All three bands played together while the black vans sulked somewhere.

"Okay, citizens. Neo here. Hold on to your hats (or something similar)," Aiden's thinly disguised voice rang out over the MemeCast. "You are not going to believe the election results—and that may be part of the reason the lights are still off in the city. Some sources say the black-out is more widespread. The juice at the compounds is beginning to waiver a bit, too. But the real news is: Mayor Albert Mignon got a mere thirteen percent of the record turnout last night. His opponent, whom nobody ever remembers is running, too, got thirty-three percent. A write-in candidate got fifty-four percent of the freaking vote. Yes, you heard right. Mayor Mignon and his Patriot Party have been defeated for their bid to get a toe-hold in Congress. And that write-in candidate is: JONAS M. WALLENBERG."

I spit-taked my juice all over the kitchen counter, and Mom just about fell off her stool. Then she started laughing.

"But wait, there's more," Aiden's voice said. "Reports are coming in from all over the country. Patriot Party candidates have been soundly defeated all over. Some with write-ins, some with real candidates—and some for Jonas Wallenberg, too."

The power flickered on a few minutes later, and Action News confirmed the fact that my dad had just won a seat in Congress. Well, he would've if he wasn't dead. TFC stock was in the toilet, and Mayor Mignon couldn't be reached for comment.

Mom started laughing again, and this time I thought she might be cracking up. Finally, she said, "Your father always liked a good joke."

"Well, the joke is on the mayor and his party." Rebecca

Starr was showing a map where the Patriot Party lost. She might as well have been showing a map of the lower forty-eight states.

"But they got the message, didn't they?" Mom texted someone as she talked.

I shrugged. Once the powers-that-be figured out Jonas Wallenberg wasn't alive, who knew what would happen. The other guy, the one that got thirty-three percent, would win, I guessed. At least it wasn't Mignon. "What message? A dead terrorist is better than a live stooge?"

"Don't you ever call your father that," Mom snapped. Then she softened. "Your dad was a hero, and don't you forget it. He fought for what he believed in. And he still—"

"Mom, I know what you told TFC—" I choked back the words.

"About how he died? I know, *mijo*, I've read all your *Memento*s." She kissed the top of my head and began clearing away the remnants of breakfast.

"But he didn't fight in the end. He left us," I said, feeling the loss and betrayal well up inside of me. He left us, and everything turned to shit. At least when I thought he was in Detention or killed, I had someone else to blame. Or I could wallow in deep denial. But now I knew the truth. "He couldn't hack it, and we ended up homeless."

Mom didn't say anything, but I could see storm clouds forming in her eyes. I felt like a douche for putting this on her. She was the one who'd fought for us. She'd worked night and day to take care of us—me. She'd lost job after job because of him. And we might lose this place now, I thought with a shudder. Yet she still fought.

"Mom, you're the hero. You stayed."

"Thank you, *mijo*," she said, drying her eyes. "The one thing you need to remember, though, is that you are not the reason your father left."

"What?" *Left?*

"*Mijo*, remember what the Meme Girl said? 'All that you remember may not be the truth,'" my mother said with a tiny smile. "It cuts both ways. All that you *forget* may not be the truth."

My groggy brain tried to grasp what she was saying.

"I've got to go, Micah." She grabbed her purse from the hook by the door. "Gotta see the Oracle about a stall." She kissed me on the cheek and then paused at the door, taking in the apartment. "How would you feel about living above Velvet and her folks?"

I shrugged, and she was off.

All that you forget may not be the truth? Did she mean the TFC memory was not the truth? Had it been changed? Or, I smacked my forehead. Had Mom *lied* to TFC—just like Velvet had? Mom told them Dad had killed himself, which meant—he wasn't dead. He'd had his own exit strategy. And Mom covered for him. Was he still out there doing his "work"? Was he coming home? Or was I totally misunderstanding everything?

I flipped on the MemeCast again while I checked my mobile on the off-chance that Dad had sent me a message, left a clue, something.

Nada.

The forums were full of buzz. Was Jonas really dead? Was he the new representative from our district? Could dead people win elections? How did he get on the ballot in the first place?

I grabbed my skateboard and headed downstairs, the greenway and Thomas Park on my brain.

As I pushed off, I recited the things I knew to be true.

Zero.

But it was enough.